The Deadliest Lead

The Deadliest Lead

A Jenna Stack Mystery

Hanna Wren

ISBN: 979-8-9878098-0-8

Cover Design: Jessie Horsting

Contents

Chapter 1
Leaving Liam

It's three a.m. The car service will be here any minute. I take a last look at the Williamsburg apartment where I've spent the last four years of my life. Maroon walls covered in vintage rock posters. The lopsided curtains I made myself, even though I can't sew. The half-full jar of change. Liam's beloved LP collection we spent weekends at flea markets trying to complete. His favorite guitar leaning against a Marshall amp. My psych books from college, stacked in the bookcase with a thousand Post-It notes sticking out. I'll have to come back for those later. On the top shelf is a picture taken the day we moved in together.

I was so happy, so in love.

I'm going to miss curling up on the window seat with our coffee Sunday mornings and taking long walks together in the afternoon.

I'm *not* going to miss bandmates crashing on the couch, dirty looks from groupies, hauling music equipment, or wondering where Liam is all night.

I pull a roller bag stuffed with clothes and my laptop over to a couple of banker's boxes jammed with my criminology books, a few framed photos, and some personal items.

Sharon, the manager of Cellos, where I bartend part time, let me leave early so I could come home and pack. I've watered the plants and left instructions. I hope they survive, but I have my doubts. Live with a rock dude, you have to expect rock dude behavior, which doesn't exactly include misting plants.

I was twenty-two when I met Liam my senior year of college. I expected a fling. But in New York, flings often turn into living arrangements. Things haven't added up for months. Tonight is just the clear answer to a series of questions. The grand, embarrassing, heartbreaking finale.

A key rattles in the lock, and Liam pushes the door open. Damn it! I was hoping to be gone before he got home.

Not surprisingly, he's been drinking. He leans against the wall, looking rumpled and sexy in black jeans and a Passion Pit T-shirt, washed so many times it barely fits his slight frame. He grins sloppily, all dimples and boyish charm. He reaches for me, then stops when he sees the bag and boxes.

"Jenna, what the...?" The look on his face is like a kid whose balloon just popped.

I walk over to the computer and tap a key. Liam's Facebook page comes up with a picture of a naked blonde strategically covered with Hello Kitty dolls. The name of his new Facebook friend is R-O-X-Y, with the "O" replaced by a heart.

"I'm not sure what's worse," I say, "her comment or her spelling."

He shakes his head and asks innocently. "She tagged me? What does she say?"

"I'll try to translate. *Thnx for last nite bad boy. Sooooo hot,*" I coo in a high-pitched voice.

"That doesn't mean anything. That's just Roxy." He feigns

confusion. "She's a girl I know. A performance artist. She's crazy." Then, as if he needs to explain her obvious appeal, he adds, "but she's into some really cool stuff."

I hold my phone up. "Yeah, she tweeted details of that cool stuff to half of New York City. You might want to show her which button is private message and which is public. There's also a picture of you two together on her Instagram. I will say one thing about her. She's thorough."

He furrows his brow and crosses his arms defiantly, like I'm the one being ridiculous.

"And at the bar tonight," I continue, "I got to field apologies from supposed friends and regulars who knew what was up and didn't say anything."

That seals the deal. He knows he's busted, and there's no denying it. He took Roxy out on the town while I was slinging drinks at Cellos, assuming no one would break dude code and tell me. What he didn't consider is the girlfriends of those dudes all live in fear they'll be publicly cheated on and humiliated the same way I've been. Once word hit Twitter, they came out of the woodwork to soothe their consciences and prove their allegiance in the hopes they won't have to suffer the same fate.

"How long have you been seeing her, Liam?" I don't know why I care. I doubt she's the first.

He shakes his head sadly. A lock of dark blond hair flops a little too strategically across his bloodshot, but still hypnotizing, green eyes.

"But Jenna..." I can see his brain working through the whiskey haze, avoiding the question, trying to come up with an argument that will have some traction. I see the exact moment—his impossibly soft lips curl up in a half smile. He thinks he has it. I can't help but be curious what his next words will be.

"We just bought a microwave!" he whines.

Seriously? If that's the best he can do, I have *soooo* made the right decision. Let Roxy have him.

"Liam, I need some time, okay?" Like a century. But I just want to get out of here.

I try to push past him with my bag. He switches his focus away from small appliances and on to his best weapon. He slouches against the wall, dejected, and looks me up and down, all brilliant eyes and pouty lips.

I open my mouth to tell him to go screw himself, or Roxy or whomever he wants, as long as it's not me and my self-respect anymore. Then he leans in, slips a finger through the belt loop of my jeans, and pulls me close.

"Come on, J," he pleads. "I need you. You're the only one for me. Pleeeasse?"

My voice catches in my throat. My outrage evaporates like a puff of steam through a subway grate, replaced by smoldering, albeit self-destructive, lust. Did I mention that Liam is infuriatingly sexy and surprisingly persuasive? Even smelling like cigarettes and whiskey, he's a force of nature. A charismatic, manipulative, stinky force of nature.

I hear three short honks outside. Saved by Brooklyn Best Car Service.

"I'll be at Dave's."

I push Liam away a little too roughly and drag the roller-bag down the stairs, half expecting him to follow me with the boxes. No luck. I race back up to grab them and find him texting on his phone. He hears me walk in.

"I'm telling her it's not cool, Jenna. Posting it. Publicly. See?"

Is he kidding? Like that's going to fix it. There's something a little crazy and sad about Liam. He is the consummate man-child, unwilling or unable to take responsibility. And tonight, Roxy has provided me with a much-needed moment of clarity—I don't want to be his mom anymore.

I close the door behind me and heft the boxes down to the waiting driver. He helps me toss them into the trunk. Then he pulls the car out into the rainy night, and we drive through the quiet streets, across the Williamsburg bridge, and into Manhattan.

As we cross the East River, the skyline twinkles. I imagine the city is welcoming me with open arms. I consider my situation. I'm single, I'm broke, and I'm technically homeless. Thank God for Dave.

Chapter 2
Tails of the City

Dave answers his door in striped flannel pajama bottoms and a white tank top. Tall, blond, chiseled, and unnaturally tan, he looks like a Bedtime Ken doll. He pulls my wet jacket off and shoves a glass of red wine in my hand.

Dave lives off Union Square in a two-bedroom apartment, second floor, no view but so chic he doesn't need one. No pets. Technically small dogs are allowed in the building, but not in Dave's place, which is ironic considering it's the world headquarters of *Tails of the City Pet Sitting Agency*.

"I ordered pad thai, chicken parm, sushi, and diner pancakes." He points to the kitchen counter, covered in take-out bags. "There's white wine, red wine, vodka, and Scotch," he counts off on his fingers, then gestures for me to sit.

Dave is always the first person I call in a disaster. I shouldn't be surprised he's spent the last two hours prepping for my arrival. Dave likes to take care of people and things. And he's been encouraging me to leave Liam for ages.

"Sit. Talk. Don't talk. What do you need?" he asks, fully engrossed in his role as caretaker.

I lift up the glass he handed me. "Right now, this is it. Thanks." I take a deep gulp of the sweet, tangy wine, feeling the warmth flood into my body, then hold the glass out for more. "Oh yeah, and the last few years of my life back, please?" I joke halfheartedly.

Dave doesn't laugh but instead looks at me sympathetically. That's all it takes. Tears start rolling down my cheeks. Damn it! I swore I was all cried out.

He puts his arms around me. "Let it go, hon."

I do just that and have a good, long, boogery cry all over his well-muscled shoulder and clean, white shirt. When it's time to blow my nose, he's ready with aloe-infused Kleenex. Honestly, he thinks of everything.

Dave and I met the first week of college and have been best friends ever since. I was there for him when he came out to his parents. He was there for me when my brother Tyler got arrested. He even came to court the day Tyler was sentenced.

We've seen each other through a long list of boyfriends, so this isn't anything new. It's just been a while since I was the one crying.

"You know I never liked him," Dave interrupts my thoughts.

"You never like anyone."

"You haven't made it easy, Jenna," he scolds. "You have atrocious taste in men."

"Don't be mean. I'm in crisis. Besides, he got the apartment!" I can't take a lecture right now or a trip down inappropriate boyfriend lane.

"Fine. But I expect you to give my opinion more weight from now on."

He's got a good point. I have made some awful choices, not the least of which was staying with Liam for so long. Although I have to say it was just in the last year, when I started fine-tuning my instincts at criminology school, that my radar really went off. Or maybe Liam began wandering when I started getting stronger and found something I was good at, something I loved more than him.

"Deal," I agree. "Although I'm off men for now."

"Me too!"

We clink glasses in a toast.

Dave recently broke up with his live-in boyfriend and some-time assistant Rob, creating a bit of a problem for Tails of the City. Rob not only screened and hired all of the help, he went out on some of the tougher jobs himself. Rob's a natural with animals. Dave, on the other hand, isn't a big pet person, which I find amusing.

Basically, Dave needed extra cash to supplement his salary at Bergdorf Goodman and fund his passion for travel. Based on the ladies he encountered at work, he suspected there was a moneyed client base willing to pay for high-end, personalized pet care.

With that in mind, he started Tails of the City two years ago. Ironically, he's done such a great job and the business is so successful that he quit his day job. Sadly, he's too busy to go anywhere.

"Take a shower. I'll make you a plate. Thailand, Italy, Japan, or U.S.?"

For some reason, pancakes sound perfect right now.

"U.S., thanks."

I head for the bathroom. A year ago, Dave decided if he was going to be at home full time, he should have a beautiful space in which to spend his days, so he redid the place into his dream apartment.

The decor is design magazine chic, a soft warm gray with carefully selected accessories and pops of blue and green throughout. The kitchen has all new modern appliances selected with Rob's love of cooking in mind. And the shower, stocked with fancy bath products, has one of those giant, high shower heads and ferocious water pressure. It's exactly what I need.

After replacing the bar smell with bergamot and lavender and the self-pity with exhaustion and relief, I pull on an old T-shirt and a pair of boxer shorts and find Dave in front of the TV. He's made up one of the two couches with sheets and a pillow and is helping himself to the sushi I rejected. I dig into the pancakes.

"Better?"

"Hmmm," I answer, my mouth full of starchy goodness. "Thanks."

He winks at me. "Any time. Stay as long as you need."

"I hope you don't end up regretting that offer."

Going back to school and practically supporting Liam so he could keep his schedule flexible for gigs has left me in a less than ideal financial situation. I have no idea how I'm going to afford the deposit on a new apartment. I might be here a while.

"We'll figure it out. I've got some ideas," Dave assures me.

A blood curdling screech shoots out of the television. What looks like a malnourished bat is being immersed in someone's kitchen sink, and the bat doesn't like it.

"What on earth are you watching!?" I ask as I shovel in another huge bite.

"Jackson Galaxy reruns. They're trying to bathe a pissed off Sphinx."

The hairless cat lets out another mind-bending shriek.

Cheeks bulging with pancakes, I can't open my mouth, so I attempt to communicate my horror with a skeptical look.

"You've never seen it?" he asks, incredulous.

I shake my head.

"Well, you're in luck. He goes around helping people with their cat problems. But it's always the people, Jenna. It's never the cat. It's hilarious, and he's a genius. You're going to love it!"

I'm more of a dog person, but I settle in. I could use a good laugh, and anything is better than thinking about my own problems.

❧

The sound of Dave's voice breaks through a vague dream. My brother Tyler is riding his motorcycle on a twisting country road. I call out to him, but he doesn't answer. I scream. He doesn't hear me. I wake up anxious and disoriented. Dave's muffled voice drifts in through the closed door to the next room.

I check my phone. It's eight a.m. I must have fallen asleep on the couch when the hairless cat stopped screaming. No texts or calls from Liam. I wonder if he called Roxy for consolation after I left?

I'd love to put a pillow over my head and go back under, but Dave's day starts early and I'm in his space. Gotta get up. I follow the scent of freshly brewed coffee into the kitchen, grab a cup, and head for his office.

This is where the designer vibe ends. Everything in Dave's office is in a state of chaos. He sits behind a big, metal 1950s schoolteacher desk, bare feet up, talking on one of those oversized telephone headsets people wore in '70s TV commercials. Where does he find these things?

He's wearing tan cargo shorts and a fitted blue T-shirt. As always, he looks clean-shaven, minty fresh, and perfectly toned. Behind him is a wall covered with photos of dogs, cats, birds, bunnies, and other animals looking ridiculous in costumes, frolicking in the country, or happily posing with their families. To his left is the job board. Active jobs are posted in bright orange, with client notes in blue. Dave waves me in, indicating I'm not interrupting, so I sit down in a chair and wait.

Dave uses his most accommodating voice. "Well, Tony is one of our newer hires."

Silence.

He makes a yammering gesture with his hand and closes his eyes as if falling asleep.

"I'll send a replacement today," he says. "Absolutely. I'll send our absolute best! Thank you."

Dave pulls off his headset and turns his full attention toward me, "Oh honey, that woman is AWFUL. She is *Miss Awful, U.S.A.* Some drama about how Tony's been walking the dog wrong."

I shoot a knowing glare over the top of my mug as I sip my coffee.

"Okay. Okay. Tony *is* a little unreliable," he smirks.

Once Rob was out of the picture, recruiting standards at Tails of the City took a drastic nosedive. Exhibit A: Tony, a cute college freshman Dave met at a bar.

"Anyway... I have a plan!" he adds.

I love a plan. I need a plan. "I'm listening..."

"Work for me!" Dave announces as if it's a new idea.

I should have seen this coming. He's been trying to get me on board since he started the business.

"Dave, you know I love animals, but I just can't. It makes me too sad." I volunteered at an animal shelter all through high school. My guidance counselor said it would look good on college applications, and I thought it would be fun. But it was hard work, and even worse emotionally.

All of those sweet, unwanted cats and dogs are victims of human abuse, irresponsibility, or stupidity. I can still see their furry faces and big eyes looking at me through mesh fences, wagging their tails, waiting.

"Stop being a baby, Jenna. You need the money. I need the help. You have tons of experience with animals. And trust me, these pets aren't sad. They have better lives than we do. They have health insurance!"

He has a point. And I do want to help Dave out. But I'm skeptical. I'm also busy.

"I don't know, I've got bar shifts, classes…"

"I'll start you with a plum assignment. You can see how it goes. I was going to give it to Tony, but if you want it, it's all yours."

"What is it?"

"Two weeks in a lovely apartment downtown. Just a few subway stops from the bar. Laundry in the unit. Cats only. Easy breezy."

Getting out of Dave's hair for a couple of weeks and making some extra money sounds pretty good.

"What would I have to do?"

"Pet the cats, scoop the litter, make sure they have food and water. Oh! And don't trash the place. Think you can handle that?"

I've never had a cat, but I've spent plenty of time with them. As long as none are screeching and hairless, how hard could it be?

"And there's a washing machine *in* the apartment?" I watch Dave carefully. That part sounds too good to be true.

"Washer *and* dryer. The client, Andrea Billingsworth, leaves today for Aspen. You can move right in."

I want to ask Dave what it pays, but with everything he's doing for me, I'd feel like a jerk. "Okay. I'm in."

"No doorman. She left a hide-a-key." He's leaning over, handing me an orange assignment slip with the address and instructions, when he pauses. "Actually… As long as you're going to be downtown, how about a teensy little favor?"

Uh oh.

"That call was from Evan Blake's assistant." He points to the phone. "Evan is a super sweet money guy, been a client for years, very well connected. He is *not* happy, and I can *not* lose him just because Tony can't figure out how to walk a dog."

Dave is one of the most generous people I've ever met, which often makes me forget that the moment anyone gives him an inch, he is laying asphalt for the mile he's about to take. His boundaries are non-existent.

"Dave, I don't have time to run all over town for you. Not with school and homework and the bar—"

"Please? It's really close to where you'll be staying and super low maintenance. Just one dog. A cute little French Bulldog named Max. Two walks a day."

I shake my head. "I'm not exactly emotionally stable these days. I don't want to let you down. Let's start small."

"Come on! Take pity on me. That damn Susie Scott has been trying to poach Evan Blake for years." He picks up a glossy Susie's PetLove brochure from his desk and waves it furiously.

Susie Scott is Dave's only real competition, his arch-nemesis. Susie's PetLove is backed by her exceedingly adoring, obscenely rich Long Island stepfather. Susie has unlimited resources and unbridled ambition. I need to tread carefully here.

"Don't you sometimes take care of the high-end clients yourself?" I try.

"The meet and greet. The instructions. Not the dog walking! Do you think Susie walks dogs herself? How would it look if Evan Blake ran into the owner of the company, walking his dog?"

"What's so special about Evan Blake?"

"Well, aside from being gorgeous... and I mean GORGEOUS." Dave picks up a *Vanity Fair* magazine, opens it to a tabbed double-paged spread, and pushes it across the desk, revealing a photo of a dozen beautiful women posing with an array of animals.

I don't get it. "Is he a drag queen?"

That gets a giggle. "No!"

I read the headline: *Fabulous Faces of the Faux Fur and Furry Friends Fête.*

"An alliteration specialist?"

"Don't be silly." He taps his finger with irritation at a line of tiny print. At the end of a long list of sponsors, I see *Tails of the City Pet Sitting Agency.*

"Oooh, that's cool!"

"It cost me five grand, but worth every penny," Dave squeals excitedly.

"What do you get for five grand?"

"Good publicity and a ticket to the cocktail reception at the event of the season. See this one with the Maltipoo? That's Fatima Ab El Malik." He points at an elegant, middle-aged woman in a navy blue, long sleeve, high-neck dress holding a small white dog. "Fatima is the crème de la crème of New York Society. This is *her* event." He pauses for effect. "And Evan Blake works for her *husband*, Sheik Mohammad Ab El Malik."

"Am I supposed to know who these people are?"

Dave sighs, exasperated. He walks over to the window and points to the skyline. "See the black glass high rise over there?" I nod. "The sheik's company, Bokra International, owns that building and a dozen more. He's one of the ten richest men in the world, and Evan Blake *manages his finances.*"

"Oh."

"Evan got me an audience with Fatima, who invited me to bid on providing pet services for the furry fête, but I was so short-staffed because of that deserter Rob I couldn't even bid. Susie Scott got the contract."

I clearly remember it was Dave who sent Rob packing, but I'm not going to get into that now. I take a closer look at the glossy photo spread. What a group. Two ladies down from Mrs. Ab El

Malik is a fierce glamazon wrapped in a horrible-looking snake. Yuck.

"Who's that?"

"Oh, that's *Cintia*. Wife number two."

"As in the sheik has two wives?" I'm confused.

"Every sheik has at least a few," he responds dismissively. "I had a personal playdate with Honey last week. I do think Fatima liked me, though. I mean, she's so much more Bergdorf's than Target."

We all know Dave is Bergdorf's. I'm guessing Susie is Target. What does that make me—corner bodega?

"Who's Honey?" I ask, skeptically.

"Fatima's Maltipoo!" he replies exasperated. "Will you do it? Please? The fête is a huge annual event. I really need to stay on Evan's good side to have any chance to bid for next year."

"Ugh." I feel my resolve dissipating. "If it's that important to you, fine. But just until you find someone else."

Dave plucks another orange job slip off the board and hands it to me.

"Okay. And Jenna, try to look nice. These are elegant people." Now that I've agreed, he's on to critiquing my appearance. "No Chuck Taylor's. No old T-shirts. And promise me you won't mess up?"

"Scout's honor," I pledge. Not that I was a Girl Scout. It's just something we say to reassure one another. Besides, it will be good to stay busy so I don't obsess on Liam and my current situation. And I can always call Dave with questions.

"And stay away from Evan Blake. No flirting. Think of him as your boss—your off-limits boss."

"Please!" I respond, envisioning the snooty, drunk, frat boy types with too much cash who crowd the bar in their suits at happy hour. "Finance guys aren't exactly my cup of tea. Besides" —I point at him sternly— "we're off men, remember?"

He smiles and hands me Blake's address and the magazine. "Take it. I have more copies!" He probably has twenty.

As I head to the living room to grab my bags, Dave calls after me in his best wicked witch voice, "You're mine now, my pretty. Took me two years to snare you, and I'm never letting go! Ha ha ha!"

Chapter 3
Feline Fiasco

I exit the 5 train at dusk. The Financial District is desolate. Wall Street feels a little like a scene from one of those horror movies where everyone dies but there's no property damage. A crush of buildings loom in the fading light—but where are the people?

I'm considering how spooky this is, and wondering how safe I am, when a clean-cut lawyer type in a suit dashes out of a revolving door and into a subway entrance. Rushing to get home before he turns into a zombie? I haven't spent much time this far downtown. I'm not sure I'm going to like it.

I find Andrea Billingsworth's apartment building easily enough, right across from a Gristedes grocery store. That will come in handy. I punch in the code for the main entrance and enter a simple lobby with a bank of aluminum mailboxes to the left and an elevator straight ahead. It feels odd letting myself into a stranger's home.

On the fifteenth floor, the hallways are cream colored, soundless, and empty. I locate the apartment, dig the hidden key out of a planter, open the door and step inside.

The smell hits me first—then the cats. When Dave said "cats," I wasn't expecting four. But here they are, all different sizes and shapes, rubbing, purring, circling, mewling. Two adorable smallish black and whites appear to be siblings. Then there's a muscular orange tabby and a beautiful gray short hair with white socks. I'll check their tags for names later. Right now I'd better get the door shut so none slip out.

The second thing I notice, aside from being a little ripe with *eau de cat*, is that this is a kick-ass apartment. The living room has a beautiful view of downtown and an enormous flat-screen TV mounted on the wall. The pink sofa, quilted throw, and zebra lampshades are a little too girly for me, but cozy and kind of offbeat, like someone's weird, hip grandma had her way with the place. The kitchen is open to the living room and a small dining nook with an old-fashioned wrought iron table and chairs.

On closer inspection, the cabinets are crammed with every appliance imaginable, including a pasta maker. Too bad I don't cook. Next to the fridge is a fully stocked bar and temperature-controlled wine cabinet. There's a note on the fridge.

"Last minute work trip.
Full fridge.
Eat - and drink - whatever you want.
PLEASE!"

Below that is another, much longer note titled, *"Instructions."* I scan the list of names, contact numbers, and precise details.

I slide open an accordion door to reveal the most coveted of all appliances in a New York City apartment—a small, stacked washer and dryer. Jackpot!

I continue my tour of my new temporary home. In the

bedroom, a fluffy white Persian stares at me defiantly from a pile of pink and white pillows. Uh oh! That brings the cat count up to five. The bathroom has a glorious full-size tub, and curled in the sink is a tiny, sweet tiger-striped kitten, bringing the cat count up to six. I'm not sure if that's even legal.

Dave's easy breezy gig is quickly turning into a feline fiasco. And what if I can't get rid of the smell? Will I get used to it?

I pull my phone out and text him: *I'm going to kill you! How many are there?!?!*

I find three litter boxes and a dozen bowls. I follow the elaborate instructions that pretty much just add up to scoop poop, change water, and feed. It takes about fifteen minutes. I set the poop bag in the hallway and open a few windows, making sure they all have screens.

Dave texts back: *6. Don't be mad.*

At least they're all accounted for, but I'm still a little peeved. I'll definitely need to keep a close eye on them. Don't want one wasting away shut in a closet somewhere.

Me: *You said this job was my easy intro!*
Dave: *It is! You don't have to walk them! And the client is gone.*
Me: *Are you kidding? Have you ever poop-scooped 6 cats? It's going to be a full-time job!*
Dave: *I'll give you a poop bonus ;)*
Me: *It's going to take more than a bonus. You tricked me!*
Dave: *I can't help it. You're so easy!*

This isn't headed anywhere productive. Besides, I've got to get over to Evan Blake's, plus I still need to change and grab a snack.

Unpacking, I realize I left a much-needed textbook in my

rented locker at school. Wolfson often assigns books that aren't available digitally, so I spent the extra money on a locker, thinking it would be nice not to have to lug books around. But I keep forgetting stuff. Although now that I'm transient, the locker might come in handy.

Keeping in mind Dave's lecture about my appearance, I kick off my tennis shoes, open my bag, and pull out the most conservative piece of clothing I own, a fitted V-neck argyle sweater, found at a thrift store back home in upstate New York last Christmas. I pair it with a gray above-the-knee skirt, tights, and the gorgeous knee-high black suede boots I bought on sale last month after a particularly good night in bar tips.

I bring my toiletries to the bathroom and evaluate what's going on above the neck. Pretty much same as always. My mousy brown hair won't grow past my shoulders. My hazel eyes don't flash anything in sunlight. My skin is fair, with a few freckles, but not enough to be a real freckle thing. Not terrible looking, just plain. I find some interesting looking volumizing gel in the cabinet and fluff the product into my hair. Then I swipe on some extra mascara and add lip tint. At least I made an effort.

I throw on a five-dollar lavender street pashmina and the leather jacket I borrowed from Sharon and haven't returned yet. I'm feeling pretty sassy. Dave would approve.

With a few minutes to spare, I grab a Greek yogurt from the fridge and sit down at the little table. A few bites in, my phone buzzes.

Dave: *Still mad?*

I forgot we were having a text war.

By now, the tabby is lying across my feet and the twins are curled up together on the table. The kitten has emerged, scrambled into my lap, and rolled into a tiny, purring, striped ball. None of them wants anything but attention, and they all seem happy. I take a picture of the pair snuggled up on the table and text it to Dave, followed by:

Me: *Actually, no. Luv from the House of 1000 Cats! XOX "Easy" J.*

Chapter 4
Meeting Evan Blake

The head of the Criminology Department at University of Manhattan, Professor Wolfson, encourages us to practice what he calls "observations" whenever possible. My observation about pet-sitting so far is it's kind of fun to see how the one percent lives, and the free food and booze are going to make the transition to my new life much easier. But if the list Andrea Billingsworth left is anything to go by, my face-to-face with pet parent Evan Blake may not be easy.

Using the map app on my phone, I easily navigate the short walk to the steel and granite monolith that is Evan Blake's apartment building. The streetlights are just beginning to turn on, and the evening air is cool and damp. I pass scaffolding, a few banks, a real estate office, and a Dunkin' Donuts.

The Financial District is a mixture of old and new architecture: cloth awnings, arched windows, heavy plate glass. It's hard to tell the office buildings from the apartments. I check the address before pushing through the double doors into a brightly lit lobby.

A young, gangly doorman wearing a red uniform with brass

buttons guards the lobby somberly. He looks down his long nose at me. His pants are three inches too short on his tall, skinny frame, revealing white socks and shiny black shoes. He has a narrow face and hangdog eyes. A name tag on his chest reads *Lloyd*.

"May I help you?"

"Hi. I'm Jenna Stack. I'm here to see Evan Blake?" Lloyd walks over to his reception desk and checks a list.

"Oh yes, you're the girl here to walk the dog. Mr. Blake had to step out. He asked that you take Maximilian for a walk and await his return." He pushes a key and a business card across the desk.

I peer at the card, confused.

"Mr. Blake's card. You'll find a map to the preferred park on the reverse."

So, we have "preferred" parks, do we? That does not bode well for my impression of Evan Blake. I start to head deeper into the building when I realize I don't know where to go. "Excuse me, Lloyd?" He eyes me disdainfully. "Which apartment?"

"Eighteen J."

After passing signs for a gym, pool, and laundry, I find a bank of elevators with shiny brass doors. I barely have time to program Evan Blake's number into my phone as I'm whisked up eighteen flights. This is definitely one of those post-9/11 redevelopment buildings meant to entice wealthy businesspeople into living downtown.

The decor is industrial chic, all metal, granite, and glass, cold but ritzy, very masculine. I pass a series of black doors and reach 18J. The key fits but won't turn. There's snuffling at the base of the door. Must be Max wanting his walk. I jiggle and twist intently. Ugh! I do not want to have to ask Lloyd for help.

"The lock can be a bit tricky." A deep voice startles me. I turn around. Standing directly behind me is a tall stranger wearing a crisp navy-blue suit. He has soft, caramel brown eyes, straight white teeth, and a dusky complexion. His hair is black and silky. His smile is disarming. A nervous flutter rushes up to my heart.

"Sorry. I didn't mean to sneak up on you." He smells exactly like cut grass and lemonade. "You're here for Max?" I nod, unable to speak. "You're Jenna, right?"

"Yes. Jenna Stack, and you're, um, Mr. Blake?"

"Call me Evan." He smiles, gently plucks the key from my hand, then patiently demonstrates, "Push in, then pull back slightly, and…" Click.

The door opens, and waiting just inside is an adorable, chubby, cream-colored French Bulldog. He stares me down, head tilted, one ear up. There's a stranger in his home, and he's not sure how he feels about it. I carefully offer a hand to sniff, like we did at the shelter when a dog seemed wary. He sniffs, then loses interest and turns his attention to Evan.

"Hey buddy. How ya doing?" Evan says. The dog jumps up into his master's extended arms and licks his face in a slobbery display of affection that Evan rewards with a big, goofy, dazzling smile. Sharon once showed me a website called *Cute Boys with Cats*. I wonder if there's one for hot men with dogs? I guarantee this image would get a lot of hits.

People meet through their pets all the time, right? It would be such a good story for the grandkids. Too bad I'm off men, and Evan Blake is off limits. He probably wouldn't go for me anyway. But it's fun to think about.

I shake myself out of the fantasy and take a glance around. The apartment is utterly fantastic and a little bit depressing at the same time. A large desk faces a wall of windows and a long balcony. An open floor plan reveals stainless steel appliances, granite counter-tops, and a professional espresso machine.

The decor is cream and gray with gleaming wood floors, but without a single knickknack or personal touch. Like it's a model home, and he's just pretending to live there. Even Max, who has trotted off to sit quietly on an area rug, looks like a prop.

Evan sets his keys on his desk and rifles through a neat stack of papers. He hands me a very long, very detailed list: favorite toys, friendly and unfriendly dogs at the park, walking routes with maps, off-limits furniture and rooms, dog gate schematics, antibacterial poop bags, approved snacks, morning food, evening food, and of course the ubiquitous contacts list. It's worse than I thought.

"Max likes a walk and a little time in the park. Afterwards he gets one treat from the blue bag and a nibble of the wheat grass."

Wheat grass. Really?

Evan picks up a lint roller and begins rolling the hair off his suit as he continues. I force myself to stay tuned to his voice. "Dr. Marchand is his vet. Dr. Franzi, his therapist."

I'm about to interrupt to ask, "Shrink, or PT?" when he hands me the roller and turns his back. "Would you mind?"

I oblige awkwardly, sneaking a sniff of him as he continues.

"Oh! And it goes without saying he shouldn't be out on the balcony alone..." And with that he turns around, blushing slightly and adds, "But I can't help saying it."

I nod, trying to reassure him that this sort of pet parent crazy is all in a day's work. Evan takes the lint roller from me and finishes up with, "Shall I email you a copy?" He may be handsome and smell good, but this guy is seriously uptight.

"That'd be great," I respond with fake enthusiasm.

Evan passes me Max's rolled-up leash.

"His lead," he says, squeezing my hand gently and looking me directly in the eyes. "I'm so glad you're here, Jenna. Thank you."

I have to stop myself from gasping. Is he flirting with me? A buzzing noise interrupts the moment.

"Mr. Blake? Mrs. Ab El Malik here to see you," Lloyd's voice drips from the intercom.

"Send her up." Evan turns to me. "Jenna, will you get the door? I'll be right back." He disappears down a hallway.

Moments later, the door opens without a knock. I recognize one of the glamazons Dave showed me this morning, live and in person.

Cintia Ab El Malik almost glows as she floats into the room. She's wearing a flowing, slightly transparent, orange tunic, skinny tan pants, and gold flats. For a moment I'm not sure she's real. This woman is perfectly put together and gorgeous. She has long, dark hair, flawless skin, and eyes a fiery shade of copper. Even with the extra effort, I'm a peasant by comparison. I'm about to introduce myself when Evan returns. Cintia greets him in a polished British accent, "Ciao, darling."

"Cintia, you are a vision." He kisses both of her cheeks, European style, lingering.

Is there a vibe here? How scandalous! Or is Evan just one of those guys who flirts with everyone?

"Didn't want to leave this with the boy downstairs," she continues, walking past me and sliding a sleek leather briefcase onto the desk. They both laugh as if it's the funniest joke ever told. I don't get it. Evan remembers they aren't alone and gestures toward me.

"Cintia Ab El Malik, this is Jenna Stack. Jenna, may I introduce Cintia."

Cintia steps closer, extending a perfectly manicured hand. A heady cloud of bergamot, cardamon, and orchid wafts through the air.

"A pleasure to meet you, Jenna."

"Jenna is here to walk Max," he adds.

My heart sinks. Suddenly, I feel like the help. Oh wait. I am. I nod and smile, jaw locked. Hi. I am the oh so average help who thought her employer might be flirting until you came along. Now I see how ridiculous that was. *What was I thinking?* "Weren't you in Vanity Fair this month? With a snake?" I blurt out.

"Yes." She lowers her eyes demurely, then shakes her head and whispers conspiratorially, "Anything for a good cause," before turning to Evan. "Don't you dare forget the fête Saturday, dear. You'd never be forgiven!"

"Biggest event of the season. I couldn't possibly forget." They smile at each other knowingly. He sure does find her amusing. "Time to go." Evan abruptly switches back to all business. "I don't want to be late to meet Abassi."

"Give Adar my love," Cintia says.

Max begins jumping up and spinning in a circle as I unroll the leash and attach the clip to his collar.

"Jenna, have you got any questions?"

"Nope. I think I've got it," I say, pulling out the card Lloyd gave me. Evan scoops up the briefcase, adjusts his tie in the hall mirror, and hustles us all out the door.

Chapter 5
Following Closely

Cintia barely has her hand in the air when two cabs fight to stop in front of her. She climbs in and waves as Evan disappears around the corner.

Okay Max, it's just you and me. I check out the meticulously drawn map to Battery Park, drafted with A+ penmanship on the back of Evan's business card. I try to lead Max toward Broadway. The problem is, he isn't the least bit interested in heading that direction. I tug on his collar, but he digs in his paws, yanking me east with all of his strength, panting, whining, and looking back at me with wide, earnest eyes.

"Come on, boy. Don't you want to go to the park?" I ask in that special baby voice reserved for pets and children.

Max dances over to a hydrant, pees, and yanks again. I give in. I know it's probably not smart to acquiesce this early in our relationship. But I'm new and temporary. And if the little guy prefers the urban landscape, who am I to deny him? He weaves back and forth, tangling me in his leash. I'm starting to see why Tony had trouble. I try everything from stern commands to gentle coaxing, but it's like dealing with a tiny canine sailor who drank too much on leave.

I finally figure out if I keep the lead short and walk with determination, he falls in line... kind of.

At the end of the block, Max turns the corner and hurries on, squat legs hustling. He seems to be on some sort of mission. Halfway down the block, I realize what's going on. He's following his master.

Evan walks briskly ahead of us, briefcase in hand, headed toward an outdoor cafe. I observe two very attractive women blatantly check him out. He doesn't respond or even acknowledge them. Either he's used to the attention or he's clueless.

Evan approaches a dark-skinned man with a bald head and neatly trimmed beard. He's wearing a gray suit with a red tie. A color-coordinated handkerchief peeks out of his breast pocket. This must be Adar Abassi. He is seated, sipping from a tiny espresso cup, reading a newspaper. His posture is stiff and formal. He nods at Evan in greeting and stands up.

"Okay boy, good dog. You've seen your daddy. Let's go." I tug, but Max strains at the leash. "What is it?" Max looks at me, ears up, panting, reaching in the direction of Evan. He starts to whine. I may not be a professional pet sitter, but I've spent enough time around animals to trust their instincts, sometimes even more than my own, and this dog is acting strange. "What's the problem, buddy?"

Looking around, I notice a handsome, tough-looking man in sunglasses and a suit talking to himself at the corner, twenty feet from the cafe. No phone, headphones, or Bluetooth. Weird. He glances right and I follow his gaze. Another guy, heavyset, with pockmarked cheeks and wearing a blue sweatshirt and a Yankees baseball cap, nods.

Are they talking to each other? Interesting.

Evan and Abassi leave the café, then sure enough, the two men follow. Professor Wolfson taught us about surveillance techniques last semester, and these two are going by the book. Max jumps wildly, and I let him pull me forward. As we follow, I take out my phone and dial Evan's number.

Up ahead, he casually pulls out his phone, looks at the screen, and puts it back in his pocket. Damn it. I don't answer phone numbers I don't recognize either.

Suddenly, the two men speed up behind Evan and Abassi. They all round the corner out of sight. Max is growling now, straining to get out of his collar. I follow, slowly and cautiously, turning just in time to see the guy wearing sunglasses force Evan and Abassi into an alley. Is this a mugging? Crap! Whatever's happening doesn't look good. What should I do?

I dial 911 and immediately get put on hold. Are you kidding me? I inch toward the alley entrance, and with one massive yank, Max pulls the leash out of my hand. "Max!" The dog isn't listening. His tiny legs churn as he runs into the alley, straight toward his master. I catch up, scoop Max into my arms, and crouch behind a trashcan.

Farther down the dark alley, Sunglasses points a gun at Abassi, who is on his knees, clutching the briefcase. Evan slumps against the dirty brick of one of the buildings, stunned. Is he hurt? Where's the other guy? The one with the baseball hat?

I'm looking around for something to throw, to make noise, create a distraction, when I'm grabbed from behind. The phone drops as Max flies out of my arms with a yelp.

A hand covers my mouth. It's him. The guy in the cap. He smells like cigarettes and sweat, and his fingernails are dirty. He shoves me into the alley, away from the street. I struggle, but he's strong. I try to think of anything I've learned from school or seen on TV. Bite. Poke out his eyes. Stomp on his foot. I can't get to his eyes, so I bite down hard on his hand and smash his foot with the heel of my boot. Max starts barking and growling, nipping at his legs.

"Stupid bitch," the man growls. What is that accent? He slams me into the brick, scattering trash cans. Then he gets me in a chokehold and ratchets up the pressure on my throat. "Scream and I kill you."

Scream? Is he kidding? I can barely breathe. Instead, I dig my nails into his forearm and claw, ripping his sleeve open. He loosens his grip a little, and I gasp for air. His arm is covered in crudely rendered tattoos. I recognize a grim reaper and what looks like military braiding on his shoulder. This asshole sure likes ink—and choking women.

"Please! Take whatever you want. Just don't hurt her," Evan calls out. Max runs straight toward his master's voice. Then the little dog leaps into the air and his jaw clamps onto Sunglasses' gun arm. The weapon flies out of his hand, hits the ground with a loud clunk, and slides across the alley to my feet.

Good dog! In the commotion, I twist and slam my attacker hard against the wall. A whoosh of air escapes his lungs. I use the opportunity to elbow him in the side. There's a nasty cracking sound. Quickly, I slip out of his grip and grab the gun.

"Back off!" I scream, pointing the gun wildly as he's catching his balance. My hand is shaking. I can tell by the smirk on his face that he's not convinced I know how to handle the weapon.

He's right. I have no idea how to shoot the thing. But I'm willing to try.

I point the gun a little high and squeeze the trigger. Bricks explode over his shoulder, showering his cap in brick dust. I level the muzzle at his gut and in a serious tone say the first thing that comes to my mind, something I heard in a movie once. "I hear it's a slow way to die."

I don't think the mugger gets the reference, but he takes me seriously and raises his hands. Under his bullish chin is a thick scar, running from the base of his left ear to the front of his throat. "You bitch! I kill you!" he spits out.

Now I recognize the accent. He's Russian. Or maybe Ukrainian. I've heard that rough, throaty sound before, the day Liam and I went to get borscht in a Russian neighborhood at Brighton Beach.

"Move," I tell him, "toward your friend."

Reluctantly, the Russian steps back toward his partner. Sunglasses looks at me. I can't see his eyes, but his jaw drops in surprise before he raises his hands too. In the dim light, an eight-pointed star tattoo is visible on his right hand, just above his knuckles.

The guy in the cap suddenly lunges toward the briefcase, but Abassi won't let go.

I swing the gun toward him and motion with the barrel. "Drop it, or I'll shoot." I'm surprised at the determination in my voice and the steadiness of my hand. I point the gun directly at the muggers. "I'm not kidding."

Sirens blare, and for the first time in my life, I am thrilled by that startling sound.

Sunglasses bolts and yells at his accomplice, "Forget it! Let's go!"

The guy in the cap drops the case and sprints toward the alley entrance. Then he draws a heavy black gun and whips around to point the barrel at Evan. Abassi dives to protect him as two shots are fired. The first bullet pings against a metal trashcan and the second bounces off the pavement. The briefcase tumbles into an oily puddle as the mugger disappears around the corner.

I run to Evan. "Are you hit?"

He shakes his head. "I'm fine."

"Why do they want that case so badly?"

"I don't know, Jenna. Adar? Are you all right?"

Abassi clutches his side and groans, a stunned expression on his face. He's been shot. Blood oozes out from under his hand. His fingers drip red. I've never seen someone get shot. It's not like the movies, no slow motion, no music—just pop and done.

The sirens are closing in as I struggle to find my cell phone. There it is, on the ground. I pick it up and the line is still open. "We need an ambulance! Send an ambulance!"

A sane, professional voice replies, "The police are on their way."

"And a goddamn ambulance! Someone's been shot!"

Abassi sinks to the cement, body heavy, face pale, breathing rapidly. He moans and grimaces, fighting off the pain.

Evan rushes over and grabs his shoulders, steadying him. "Adar? Hold on, help is coming. Adar?" He looks at me, frantic, unsure what to do.

I kneel down and put the gun to one side. "We need pressure on that wound." I start to peel away Abassi's coat. Evan helps me pull away his blood-soaked shirt. The bullet hit him in the ribcage, but the blood is seeping, not pulsing, which I'm pretty sure means it missed any major arteries. I take off my scarf and press the cloth against the wound. The bleeding slows down.

Max jumps on Evan, licking him and whining, but Evan looks like he's in a trance.

"Are you okay?" I reach over and grab his shoulder. Evan touches his hair and finds blood on his hand. He nods.

"I just hit my head. I'm okay, I think."

The mouth of the alley is filling up with bystanders and looky-loos peering in to see what's going on. Then a black and white cruiser pulls up, followed by an ambulance. A pair of cops jump out and race toward us. I feel woozy.

Evan shakes his head with disbelief, finally registering what just happened, "He—he saved my life." He looks down at Abassi and takes his hand gently. "Hang in there, Adar."

Chapter 6
The First Precinct

Detective John Denning sits across from me at a dented metal desk, slowly tapping a pencil and frowning. First, I catch my boyfriend cheating. Then I witness a mugging and shooting. Now I'm in a police station at ten at night. Could this week get any worse?

Despite the fluorescent lights overhead, the room is filled with shadows. Denning's desk is spartan, with a beat-up old computer, a banker's light, and a dozen files scattered across a beige blotter scrawled with notes. Behind him, a sad, dirty window faces onto a brick wall.

Denning looks like he just came back from a casting call for attractive, disheveled detectives. In my experience, most real cops look like they live on a steady diet of burgers and fries, but not Denning. He's six feet tall, good looking, and fit. He runs his free hand through messy, dark blond hair in frustration. His hands are rough, like someone who fixes his own car or builds things. He narrows his blue eyes as he examines the report in front of him.

He's tired but not giving up. The questions that seemed helpful an hour ago have devolved into what feels like an interrogation.

"What were you doing in the alley?" he asks. "How many times did you shoot the gun? What did the other guys look like?"

Everything started to go south when Denning pried open the briefcase and found $100,000 stuffed in the lining. The stunned expression on Evan's face, followed by the word *courier*, led to a marathon of questions.

To a cop, a secret lining stuffed with more money than he'll make in a year is like waving a shiny diamond ring in front of a magpie. He's relentless. "Did you know there was money in the briefcase?" he asks me for the tenth time.

"No, I didn't. How would I?"

"How do you know Adar Abassi?"

"I told you. I don't know him. But Adar Abassi is the victim here, and as far as I'm concerned, he's a hero."

"I'd be careful about making those kinds of assumptions, Miss Stack."

"Look, Detective, I've told you everything I know. I'm tired. I want to go home. Don't you have to go to the forensics lab or something?"

He shoots me a nasty look.

I hate feeling trapped at a police station. It reminds me of the night Tyler was booked. Sheriff Wade Parker's endless reaching questions, repeated over and over as if Ty was stupid, or the answers were going to change. Denning has that same stubborn quality.

At another desk, Evan is seated, under the watchful eye of a no-nonsense lady cop, with Max sleeping in his lap. He shoots me a weary glance.

"So your attacker had tattoos and a Russian accent? Anything else about these *muggers*?" Denning emphasizes muggers as if they're a figment of my imagination.

"I've already told you ten times. One was in sunglasses, the other had a cap, they both had handguns. They seemed like professionals."

"That's the thing, Miss Stack. Your descriptions are awfully detailed, considering you only saw them for a minute."

"I have a good memory."

"Mr. Blake's descriptions were more vague."

"Yes, but similar, I'm sure. And please, call me Jenna."

Denning waits, staring at me calmly as if I'm supposed to question what Evan said. But even if his version conflicts with mine, I'm not worried. Eyewitness testimony is notoriously unreliable, and I know what I saw.

Denning lets the silence drag on. I can't take it and follow up with an explanation. "I'm enrolled in the criminology program at University of Manhattan. I know what to look for."

He's good. That's a classic interrogation technique. Most people, myself included, can't stand long pauses. But I don't think that was exactly the big reveal he was looking for.

"Wolfson?"

"Um, yeah." I sometimes forget Professor Wolfson is famous for pioneering the field of criminology. He's on CNN all the time.

"I had him. Has he played that stupid card trick on you yet?"

"Card trick? Not yet."

"He will."

"He did give me an A for observation and retention on my last midterm." There. The great and powerful Wolfson says I'm good with details. That should shut him up.

"Well, in that case, let's move on to mug shots."

Ugh! That just backfired. I'll be stuck here all night.

Denning gets up, presumably to fetch mug shot books or set up a room for me to look at them. He has an athletic gait. I'm not sure if he saunters or swaggers, but he moves like a man in control. I bet he's from a long line of cops.

As Denning walks past an open office, a man with a receding hairline and a thick waist motions him inside. They're behind a glass partition, but the conversation looks heated. Denning rubs his chin and shakes his head. The other man, clearly his superior, stands his ground. Denning storms back over to the desk like a petulant child.

"You're free to go." He shoves a business card at me. "Good luck with Wolfson."

Huh?

He looks at Evan. "You too."

The lady cop is just as confused as we are.

"What's going on? Did you find out something?"

Denning looks at me. I can tell he isn't pleased.

"It seems we have a jurisdictional conflict."

"But this is the first precinct. The crime happened on your turf. How could there be a conflict?"

"In case you hadn't noticed, Miss Stack, you're still in school and I'm a detective. Why don't you leave the police work to the professionals?"

"Who has the case now?"

"That's none of your concern," he replies brusquely.

"But how will we know what's happening?"

"Oh, you'll know." He motions toward the exit. Evan and I both make our way through the maze of cubicles and out the front door. I'm not sure what just happened, but I'm glad to be out of the rundown squad room.

The night air feels fresh after being cooped up for so long. Evan seems lost in thought. I guess he's still pretty shaken up. He sets Max down as we start walking instinctively away from the station.

"I don't know how to thank you, Jenna," Evan says.

"Thank Max. He led me right to you. I think he knew you were in trouble." I reach down and pat his tiny head.

Max wags his tail and circles around Evan's legs, forcing him to step in and out of the leash. "Can I get you a cab?"

"I have an errand to run uptown. I'll hop on the train, but thanks."

"See you tomorrow?"

"Nothing keeps a dog walker from her duty." Ugh. That was corny. I leave Evan and Max on the corner, thinking to myself, this has been the strangest first day on a job that I've ever had.

Chapter 7
Central Park at Night

Down in the dim light of the subway station, I lean against a pillar and rest my eyes for what seems like only a second before the tracks start to rattle. The telltale hot breeze of the oncoming train blasts my face. Good timing for a change.

The train heads into the station, sending rats scurrying from the tracks. It slows to a stop. The doors open with a groan, and I step inside. The car is half full of workers on their way to graveyard shifts and night owls heading out on the town. I find a seat and settle down for the ride.

Even though I'm beyond tired, I need to make a quick stop at U of M and pick up that textbook, *Crime and Human Nature,* from my locker. There's a test on the material tomorrow and I need to cram in the morning.

With every subway stop, more people board the train until there are no seats left. A pregnant woman gets on board. When no one offers her their seat, I stand up and lean against the door dividing the cars as the train rocks back and forth.

That's when I catch a flash of a reflection from the car ahead. I squint to see where it came from. The reflection is from a pair of sunglasses. Who wears sunglasses in the subway at night?

It's the thug from the alley. I fight back panic. Did he wait outside the police station? Follow me? How did I miss him? How many times has Wolfson reminded us to be aware of our surroundings? It's my own fault. A cop station seemed safe—I let my guard down.

As the train pulls into the next station, I check the numbers flashing by on the tile wall—72nd Street. The platform is crowded. The doors slide open. I wait a heartbeat.

Just before they slide shut, I slip through the gap and out onto the platform. I look over my shoulder and see an arm thrust through the closing doors of the next car. He was ready. I push my way through the people milling on the platform, hoping he'll lose sight of me.

I run as fast as I can up the stairs, taking the steps two at a time. At the top, I race across the sidewalk, almost toppling a man walking his beagle. At the curb, I jump up and down, trying to hail a taxi. No luck. One seems to slow down, so I step into the street, waving my arms. The cab cuts through a puddle, spraying me with dirty water, and continues down the road.

Then Sunglasses bursts up from the subway entrance. Too proud to die trying to hail a cab, I run for it, cutting across traffic. I realize I've made a grave error. Cars start honking, drawing attention exactly where I don't want it—on me. I weave through traffic and find myself facing an entrance to Central Park. Heavy clouds have rolled in from the east, darkening the skies.

Isn't there an unwritten rule about never entering Central Park at night? I glance back to see Sunglasses halfway across the road. At this moment, the shadows and trees look a lot more like a refuge than a threat.

I run straight into the park and down a winding path. My

lungs are burning as I duck behind a tree to catch my breath. I try my phone. No service. Are you messing with me, universe? I shove the phone back in my pocket and work up the nerve to peek back.

A figure stands silhouetted against the streetlights just inside the entrance. It's him, standing still with military precision, head cocked, listening. Then he breaks into a quick jog, heading straight in my direction. I bolt and run deeper into the park, veering off the path onto uneven ground punctuated by bushes and trees. My boots are made for fashion, not hiking. Branches scratch at me as twigs and leaves get tangled in my hair. My heart is pounding. I'm too scared to look back, but I can hear crunching twigs as he races to catch up.

There's a loud ripping noise as the coat I borrowed from Sharon catches on a thorny branch. I pull free and push ahead. The park is getting darker, swallowing me. This is how it happens. One day you're hanging out with six cats eating yogurt, the next day you're in the morgue. I can see the papers now: "Random girl riding the subway with a thousand other New Yorkers found floating face up in Central Park Lake." Where are the police or the neighborhood watch, or the dorks who dress up as superheroes, when you need them? Does anyone even patrol this park? How about a horse cop? I could use a horse cop right now. I'd even call that jerk Denning if my phone would work. I push through the brambles and connect back to a path. I can run faster on even ground.

Ahead, a group of skateboarders, about fourteen years old, are practicing their moves under a lamppost. They're at an intersection where three paths branch out in different directions. I have an idea. I search my pocket and fish out some cash. I motion to one of the kids, who tucks his board under one arm and jogs over. His friends follow. I hold out a twenty.

"A guy is coming down that path." I thumb behind me. "I need you to tell him I went left."

The kid looks me over suspiciously. "You a cop?"

"Do I look like a cop?"

"Nah. You look like a hooker who just did it in the bushes."

His friends laugh. I don't have time to argue.

"Do we have a deal?"

"Tell some freak you went left? I'll do it for forty."

I'm not exactly in a position to negotiate. I empty my pockets and come up with thirty-five.

"That's all I've got. Please?"

"Cool." The kid plucks the bills from my fingers, flips his board down, and goes back to skating.

I take off to the right. The path has a steep incline curving around a maintenance building with an electric junction box outside. The current makes a loud buzzing noise. A discarded metal pipe, weapon size, lies on the ground under the box. I pick up the pipe and head into the brush to stake out a spot. Down below, the kids are flipping their boards up, practicing mounts and dismounts.

I hunker down to watch, clutching the metal pipe, trying to catch my ragged breath.

Sure enough, my pursuer comes jogging up the path and into the circle of light. Unbelievably, he still has his shades on. Are they some kind of tactical glasses? The kid I paid ignores him. Good move, kid. I can just make out what they're saying.

"Anyone come down the path?" he asks in an accent similar to his buddy's but not as thick.

"Why do you want to know?"

"I need to talk to her."

I bet you do, you crazy psycho. I try to will Sunglasses to lose interest.

The kid dutifully points down the left-branching path. Relief floods my mind as my pursuer heads in that direction.

I start to back away while keeping my eyes on him. Suddenly, he stops.

No, no, no. I hold my breath. He looks like he's sniffing the wind. He steps off the path abruptly and cuts across the grass to the right. You've got to be kidding me. Then he pulls out a gun and clicks the safety back. How many guns does this guy have?

Maybe if I just wait and don't make any noise, he won't come all the way up the path. I crouch back down, hugging the metal pipe. My beautiful, brand new, barely worn suede boots are covered in mud. An ember of rage smolders inside of me. Not only is this guy trying to kill me, he's ruined my boots! And they were the last pair in my size on sale. I try to quiet my breathing and focus on my surroundings.

His shoes make a soft clicking noise on the cement as he creeps up the path. I try to make myself smaller. Maybe he'll walk past. Please walk past. My breath sounds incredibly loud in my ears. I'm trembling and feel faint. I desperately want to bolt and run for it. But it's too late. All I can do is wait. Just as he's about to pass by me, he stops. Unbelievable! I peek through the foliage. He kneels down at the exact place I stepped off the path and picks up a broken dandelion. Seriously? I'm being chased by some sort of super tracker?

Looking around in desperation, I notice a sandy patch leading around to some waste bins. As he follows my trail, examining every broken blade of grass, I quietly step onto the sand which masks the sound of my steps. I grip the pipe tightly and double back around, brushing the surface behind me to hide my trail. As I press past the bins and behind a tree trunk, a twig snaps. He looks up, trying to determine the direction of the sound. He's moving quickly now. He's only a few yards away. I try not to breathe.

As he inches past the bins, a strange sensation comes over me. The fear drains away and is replaced by fierce determination. I am not going to die tonight in the bushes in Central Park in my ruined boots just because I saw this guy mug someone. Time slows down. My body switches to autopilot.

I step out from behind the tree and swing the pipe toward his head as hard as I can. There is a sickening thud as the pipe connects with his skull. He stumbles in a circle, arms out and looks at me, but I can't see his eyes behind the oily sheen of his sunglasses.

On his right hand is an eight-pointed star tattoo, just above his knuckles. The memory of being choked by his partner in the baseball cap, also covered in tattoos, floods back.

This time, I hit Sunglasses hard on the back of the knees, sending him to the ground stunned. He's still breathing but not moving. I kick him, softly at first, then harder. There's no reaction, so I quickly snatch the gun and search his pockets.

I switch off his phone and toss it aside. Phones can be traced. I find his wallet and flip it open. There's a Nevada driver's license issued to a Dimitri Solonik. The picture and the thug match. What's more, Solonik is loaded. I thumb through the bills in amazement. He has at least a thousand dollars in cash. My next pair of boots are on you, jerk.

I shove the wallet in my bag and head back down the path, gun in hand. Being armed, even if you don't know how to use it, is a confidence builder. I keep to the shadows and scan the path. The kids are still skating, oblivious.

I try to sort out in my head where I am in the park, but it's useless. I find a path and hope I'm heading east or west, which will get me out of here much more quickly than north or south.

Knowing I'm going to hit a street at some point, but wanting to keep the gun close at hand, I tuck it in my waistband. Before long,

I spot the back of the Metropolitan Museum of Art. I'm definitely headed east. Thank goodness. I'm almost out of here.

When I see the street up ahead, I run as fast as I can until my lungs feel like they're going to burst and emerge into the glowing streetlights of 5th Avenue. A bus is just pulling away from the curb. I run across the sidewalk, nearly stumbling into the gutter, and bang on the door. Air brakes hiss as the bus jolts to a stop. The door opens.

The driver, slumped over with gray whiskers and rheumy eyes, looks at me dryly. Breathing hard, I dig my metro card out of my pocket, swipe it, then sink gratefully into a seat. I watch the park as the bus pulls away, then take stock of my situation.

First off, what bus am I on? And where's it going? The sign says M4. Good news. This will take me straight to Penn Station, where I can switch to a downtown subway.

Now how about me? If the reaction of my fellow passengers is any indication, I must look pretty bad. An older woman pulls her bag closer to her chest, trying not to meet my eyes. A kid with a hip-hop outfit, complete with graffiti-style writing, droopy pants and hoodie layered over baseball cap, slides to the edge of his seat in case he needs to bolt.

I catch my reflection in the bus mirror. Mud is spattered across my chest and drying unpleasantly on my face. My arms and legs are full of scrapes. By tomorrow, I'll be covered in bruises. I stretch my limbs. Nothing is broken or punctured. Sharon's coat is ripped from shoulder seam to armpit. Great. Sharon is going to finish the job the Russian started. My tights are shredded spiderwebs, and my boots are soaked through and crusted with mud. I look like a bog monster. Dimitri Solonik's gun is shoved uncomfortably down the front of my underwear. Although, considering the situation, the sensation of cold metal is reassuring.

And finally... it hits me. What the hell? Why is a random

mugger, of whom there are hundreds in this city, wasting his time trying to kill a witness? And where was his buddy? Is there something more going on here? Evan! I've got to warn him. I pull my phone out and check the little service bar. We are back to civilization! I hit redial. Please answer this time.

"Um, hello?" His voice is guarded.

"Evan? It's Jenna. Listen, we've got a problem. Where are you?"

"Across the street from my building. Why?"

"You're just getting home?"

"Max and I stopped at the store. We got back a few minutes ago." He sounds weird. Distracted.

"What's wrong?"

"I'm probably just being paranoid, but there's someone standing out front, like he's waiting for something. I haven't seen him around before and he just doesn't look right. Kinda... scary."

"Listen, Evan, you need to leave right now." I'm feeling more and more paranoid myself.

"Leave? But—"

"I'm serious, Evan. You have to trust me. I'll text you an address and where to find a key. Don't let that guy see you. I'll meet you as soon as I can."

"But I still have Max. What should I do with him?"

"Bring him."

"Shouldn't we call the police?"

"Not yet. Something weird is going on. I'll see you soon." I hang up before he has a chance to object, then text him the address.

The lady across from me clutches her bag tighter and slides closer to the window. Every time another passenger makes eye contact with her, she nods her head in my direction, warning them of my presence. The hip-hop kid has lost interest and is scrolling through his phone. Good old New York.

I'm starting to register a very bad feeling. There's more to this than just a mugging. Is Evan involved somehow? In danger? Or was he just, like me, in the wrong place at the wrong time?

Chapter 8
A Big Bite of Heaven

I walk into Andrea Billingsworth's apartment to find Evan sitting on the pink couch, hair wet, wrapped in a pink bathrobe. There's a pile of used tissues on the table next to a box of Kleenex. Evan is surrounded by cats. They're snuggled up to him on the couch, lounging across his lap, purring at his shoulder. His nose is red, and he's covered in cat hair. Max is snoring at his feet, unperturbed by the scene.

He looks at me and his jaw drops. He's just as surprised by my mud-encrusted, disheveled appearance. I start to laugh, a hearty, tear-inducing, gut-wrenching laugh. That triggers him, and he starts laughing too. I struggle to catch my breath and say something, but he beats me to it.

"I was filthy. I hope you don't mind," he says, then sneezes. I can hear the washing machine running in the background. "And I'm allergic," he explains. "What's your excuse?"

I fish the wallet I took from Solonik out of my pocket, then open it and place it on the coffee table. "Pretty decent picture of our friend. Don't you agree?"

Evan picks up the wallet and studies the ID. "Yes, it is."

"Nevada license. Says his name is Dimitri Solonik."

"How did you get this?"

"I was followed and attacked."

"By Solonik?" He looks at me with genuine concern. "Are you okay, Jenna?"

"No permanent damage. Just freaked out."

Max stretches and pads off into the bedroom as Evan gets up from the pile of cats. He pulls me into the kitchen and looks me over for wounds. "Here. Sit. Tell me what happened."

He pulls out a chair for me and places the wallet on the table. Then he holds a fresh dish towel under the faucet. As he cleans the cuts on my arms, I'm reminded of the way my mom used to tend Tyler's and my little boo-boos when we were small.

Evan's robe drapes opens, revealing polka dot boxer shorts. He's not the least bit self-conscious about his lack of clothing. Odd for such a fastidious guy. Then again, he's got nothing to worry about. He's definitely not skipping the gym. He picks a twig out of my hair.

"Solonik was also carrying this." I pull the gun out and slide it to the center of the table.

"You got his wallet and gun?" Evan looks at me, astonished. "How?"

For some reason I feel a little embarrassed.

"I disarmed him." I shrug.

"*You?* But you're so, so—"

"So what?"

"Small."

"Honestly, I don't know exactly. I had an adrenaline surge or something. Anyway, I took Krav Maga last summer."

"How many lessons?"

"Three. But as soon as I get some money, I'm signing up for the whole course. I also smacked him in the head with a pipe, which helped."

Evan looks impressed or stunned, I'm not sure which. He starts dabbing at my cuts again, but I grab his wrist and force him to make eye contact.

"Now would be a good time to tell me if you're in trouble. Or into anything illegal."

He shakes his head, pulls a chair out, and sits down next to me. "No, Jenna, I swear! My job isn't dangerous or sinister. I don't gamble or fraternize with shady characters. I'm a money manager, a glorified accountant. I'm just as confused by this situation as you are."

He seems sincere.

"All right then, how often does Abassi pick up money from you?"

"Maybe twice a month."

"Who knows about the pick-ups?"

"A whole office full of people. Adar is our primary Hawala courier."

"What does that mean exactly?"

"Hawala is an ancient banking system that uses a network of couriers to deliver money and valuables. Think of it as kind of like making a wire transfer—in person."

"That's insane."

"Not really. It's an extremely efficient way to move money quickly and quietly. It's done all the time." Evan has a strange way of switching back and forth between robot-like and human.

"Is it legal?"

"Of course it's legal."

"Sounds shady to me."

"It can be. Some people use it for illicit transactions. The strange thing is, my employer, Sheik Mohammad Ab El Malik, insists we never move more than ten thousand dollars in cash. That's the Bokra International policy. For larger amounts, we use letters and pay the funds out at the other end."

"Then why was there a hundred grand in the briefcase today?"

"I don't know."

"Who had access?"

"The list varies with each shipment, but the briefcase is always sealed at the office. Sometimes only the sheik knows what's inside."

"Could the sheik be behind this?"

"Mohammad? He's not one to break rules, particularly his own."

I'm not sure anyone who orders, receives, hands off, or sends briefcases full of valuables on a regular basis can be trusted, including Evan.

"Don't you worry this system is dangerous?"

"I never have a shipment for long."

"But what about Adar?"

"Adar is well trained and very careful. He moves money, papers, jewels, all kinds of things all the time. I can't believe he didn't notice we were being followed."

"They were professionals, Evan. People like that don't guess. They must have known Adar had something worth stealing."

He nods, agreeing with my logic.

"How well do you know your boss?"

He smiles broadly. "The sheik was my dad's closest friend. After my father passed away, I stayed with the Ab El Maliks on school holidays while my mother ran around with her husband du jour. Mohammad helped me get into college and steered me toward a career in finance. I even introduced him to Cintia, who was a classmate. So, I'd say I know him pretty damn well. We're like family. Whatever is going on, he's not involved."

Evan seems certain, but I wonder if his relationship with the sheik hasn't clouded his judgment. I'll leave it alone for now. I want to believe in Evan, to trust him. I just don't have enough facts to draw any conclusions beyond the obvious one. Something isn't right. Time to change the subject. "Do you drink?"

He nods. I walk to the cabinet and pull out an expensive bottle of Tequila. I set up two glasses, then pour and take a swallow. A pleasant heat rises up from my belly.

"How many husbands, total?"

"My mother?"

"Yes."

"She is currently divorcing number four."

My eyes widen involuntarily.

"Don't get me wrong," he continues. "She's great. Just prone to infatuations. What about you?"

I take another sip of Tequila. Evan and I certainly come from two different worlds. He grew up privileged, while the Stacks struggled.

"Well, let's see. My dad left when I was little, and my mom never remarried. I have one brother. How about you? Any siblings?" No need to tell him the saga of Tyler so early into our friendship.

"I was an only child." Evan smiles, aware of the difference between us as well. The pause drags on. We've run out of casual conversation. Evan breaks the silence.

"What about Detective Denning? Shouldn't we call him? Tell him about Solonik?"

I shake my head. "You can try. But I don't know if he can help us. Something strange was going on at that precinct, as if they were trying to bury the case."

"Why would they do that?"

"I don't know, Evan. But I think we're on our own." My stomach growls loudly. "Excuse me."

"Why don't you get cleaned up?" Evan suggests. "I'll scrape up something to eat and make a few calls."

While gathering a change of clothes, I discover Max asleep on the bed in a little cream-colored ball. I'd forgotten about Max! He immediately wakes up and starts running in circles.

"Good boy." I scratch behind his ears. "Sorry buddy. You're bunking with the cats for a while."

I take a hot shower but keep it short, then slip into yoga pants and a tank top.

When I emerge, the tissues have been cleaned up and the Tequila put away. In its place is a bottle of chardonnay. The little kitchen table is set for dinner and the room smells like herbs and garlic. There's a beautiful frittata and a mixed green salad set out on the counter. The pink robe is gone, and Evan's slipped back into a clean T-shirt and slacks. His nose is still slightly red, but it almost makes him sexier.

I slide onto a chair, trying to remember a time a man cooked for me on a normal day, much less mid-crisis or mid-crime. This is a first.

He gestures at the spread awkwardly. "I cook when I'm nervous."

"I drink when I'm nervous," I say, smiling, and pour a glass of wine. We dig in. I'm ravenous. I haven't eaten since breakfast. "This is so delicious."

"You're just really hungry." He blushes.

"Is this dressing homemade?"

"My signature vinaigrette," he beams. "I love food. I always secretly wanted to be a chef and have my own restaurant."

I take another big bite of heaven.

"Why didn't you?"

"I don't know," he replies wistfully. "I guess I didn't think my family would approve of me going into... service."

"What's wrong with service?" I try not to sound insulted, but my voice jumps an octave.

Evan's face drops.

"I'm so sorry, Jenna. I didn't mean it like that. Really. Can you forgive me?"

"Forget it." I guess he doesn't spend much time with bartenders or dog walkers.

There's another silence, this one uncomfortable. Then Evan switches the subject.

"I spoke to the hospital."

"Is Adar okay?"

"Yes. He's out of surgery and recovering."

"We should talk to him. Find out what he knows."

"He's allowed visitors in the morning. I also spoke to Mohammad. He's just as concerned as we are. He insisted on sending security to my building tomorrow. I can also have someone sent here," he suggests.

I consider his offer. Yes, I'm concerned, even scared, but no one knows where I am except Dave and now Evan. I'm not even sure it's smart for Evan to know.

"I think it's best if you don't mention tonight to the people you work with, not until we know more."

"Then you could come stay with me, starting tomorrow," Evan suggests. "I mean if you feel scared. I have room. And I'll be working from home the next few days."

As tempting as that sounds, I'm not letting a pair of thugs rearrange my life.

"No. I'll be fine. Just stay here tonight and we'll go talk to Adar in the morning, see if he has any idea what's going on." I dig some allergy tablets out of my purse and hand them to Evan. "You'll need these. The cats are going to want to cuddle."

Evan smiles, accepting the meds. He begins clearing and washing the dishes. If he's secretly in on the caper and kills me in my sleep, at least I got waited on hand and foot my last night on earth.

Surprised to find the wine bottle empty, I uncork a fresh bottle of pinot noir. Dave can buy Andrea Billingsworth a case of wine after what I've been through. I let the vino breathe while I curl up on the couch and start flicking through TV channels.

As soon as Evan finishes cleaning up, he slides next to me. "I'm really sorry if I sounded like a jerk, Jenna."

"It's okay."

He refills our glasses. "To new... friends?"

"And getting to the bottom of the mystery." We clink glasses.

After a few minutes, he puts his arm around me and gently draws me toward him. With his hand lightly stroking my shoulder, he nuzzles the top of my head and whispers, "Don't worry. We'll figure this out tomorrow. You're safe tonight."

Buzzed and sated with delicious food, electricity coursing through my body from his touch, I lay my head on his chest, just for a minute. Feels so good. He lets out a sigh.

The next thing I know, I wake up, in bed, next to Evan. I panic and sit bolt upright, waking Max, who is nestled at the foot of the bed. The clock says four a.m. My head is throbbing from too much wine. I check under the covers. Evan is still wearing his T-shirt and boxers from last night. Okay. That's a good sign. I check myself. I'm fully clothed.

Evan rolls over and smiles. "Give me some credit. You passed out. I carried you in here. I'm nothing if not a gentleman."

I feel myself blush. "Sorry."

He pulls me toward him and spoons me. Max settles back down. "That's okay. I did think about it," he teases.

My heart thumps loudly in my chest. I try to drift off but can't fall back asleep. Once Evan's breathing steadies, I slip out from under the covers and into the kitchen. I wake up my laptop and start googling: Bokra International, Hawala, and Sheik Mohammad Ab El Malik. Everything Evan told me checks out.

Next, I search for tattoos. The braided design on my attacker's shoulder is called an epaulet and is common among gangs in Eastern European prisons. So is the star tattoo, sometimes gang related, denoting master thieves connected to the Russian mob. On the knees, those stars mean "I kneel to no man."

Finally, I search Evan's name. Based on the results, his life is as straightforward as he claims. He grew up affluent and educated, private schools and summer houses. He sure is a charmer. And maybe because of that, I still don't entirely trust him.

Chapter 9
Eleven West Wing

The retreating steps of an orderly echo through the cool halls of Mount Sinai Hospital's Eleven West wing.

A private security guard wearing a dark suit is stationed outside Adar Abassi's room. His eyes move constantly, scanning the halls. As we approach, he recognizes Evan and holds open the door. We enter a scene I wasn't expecting. Floor-to-ceiling windows offer a panoramic view of the East River. In the distance, green treetops sway against a crisp blue sky. The vista is framed by heavy curtains, deep plum with gold stripes. The same colors are reflected in the upholstery of a plush couch and cozy-wing chair, forming a small reception area.

Seated in the chair is another guard, this one wearing a holster with a gun.

A violin concerto plays softly from a small speaker on a mahogany end table. Heavy books on an array of topics are stacked on a coffee table. A bar cart with crystal glasses, decanters, and bottles of booze is tucked neatly to one side. Lamps cast a soothing yellow glow. This is a world I didn't know existed. The finest hospital room money can buy.

Beyond the luxurious reception area, Adar Abassi is propped up in a hospital bed, his chest bandaged, one arm in a sling. There are faint iodine stains where his ribs are still tightly bandaged. The decor and ambiance of his "bedroom" are coordinated with the reception area.

Abassi spent the night in critical condition and in the morning was moved to this exclusive wing of the hospital. A heart monitor is clipped to his finger, measuring his pulse on a screen. He reads a newspaper, his glasses perched low on his nose. When he sees Evan, he smiles, folds up his *New York Times*, places it neatly aside, and returns his glasses to a leather case on the bedside table.

Abassi is impeccable, even when incapacitated. His robe is pressed, his beard neatly groomed. If it weren't for his condition and the medical equipment, I would think him a wealthy businessman relaxing in a four-star hotel suite before starting his day.

Prior to Cellos, I worked at Bellevue Hospital, assisting PTSD therapy groups. I was only there for six months before being laid off, but it made an impact, like a blast of depressing, gritty reality, cruelly bursting the last of my college bubble. Most of my patients were veterans, victims of violent crime or people trying to come to grips with their horrific dreams and debilitating memories. The grimy chairs of the waiting room were choked with the homeless. Patients injured during arrest were patched up and handcuffed to their beds. Whenever I passed the ER, the wounded called out or waved their hands to draw attention to their plight. Compared to that, even an average room at Mount Sinai is an upgrade. Abassi's room is sheer decadence, and a bit unnerving.

An extravagant floral bouquet masks a pungent undercurrent of antiseptic. Abassi can press a button to signal for help that will actually arrive shortly. I imagine he can also order a manicure or a massage. This room must cost thousands of dollars a day. What do couriers make? Is the sheik paying for this? And those guards? That's a health plan I'd like to get on, please.

Evan nods to the second security guard as he approaches Abassi's bed. I follow and wait a few steps away. He glances at Abassi's bandages. "How are you feeling?"

"The bullet shattered a rib but missed my heart. I'm alive and anxious to get out of here," Abassi replies in a clipped British accent, not unlike Cintia's. "How's that monstrous little dog of yours?"

"That little dog helped save your life, Adar. And he's unscathed, thank you."

Adar nods, smiling. "Yes. I am grateful."

"I owe you a debt of gratitude, Adar. If you hadn't pushed me out of the way, I'd be here too." Evan gestures at the room. "Or worse."

"It's not so bad here, old friend. I could pretend it's a vacation if it weren't for the company." He tilts his head in the direction of the guards.

"I'm afraid that might be my fault. I called Mohammad. But two guards does seem excessive."

"You know Mohammad," Adar responds. "Better safe than frugal." They chat like a couple of school chums. "And you Evan, always lax with the manners." He tilts his head toward me.

"Ah, of course. May I introduce my friend, Jenna Stack? You were unconscious at the time, but her quick thinking contributed to you not losing all of your blood in that alley."

I extend my hand to Abassi. We shake.

"An honor, Miss Stack. Thank you."

I have definitely been hanging with the wrong crowd. I could get used to being around all of these courteous, attentive men.

"Mister Abassi," I say, "may I ask you a few questions about yesterday?"

"Of course." Abassi smiles and waves his hand as if I've earned that much.

"Did you know the men who attacked you?"

He shoots Evan a stern glance before answering brusquely. "Of course not."

Nice start, Jenna. You've insulted him. Or he thinks you're an idiot.

"Evan explained you're a courier." I avoid using the word Hawala. I'm not sure why. It just seems prudent to be vague. "Where were you taking the briefcase?"

Abassi glances at the security guard in the living room, then disapprovingly at Evan before looking directly at me.

"What business is that of yours?"

Evan interrupts. "They tried to kill her, too. We're just trying to get to the bottom of this."

"Who tried to kill you?" Abassi demands.

Evan continues, answering for me, "One of the muggers chased her last night."

Abassi furrows his brow. He seems genuinely perplexed. "And how do you fit into this?" Evan draws a breath to talk but I interrupt.

"I don't. That's the thing. I'm just the pet sitter." I appreciate Evan introducing me as his friend. But I think it's relevant to share that I'm coming late to this not-so-fun party. "It was a coincidence I was even there. But one of the men followed me from the police station, after we gave our statements."

"Followed you? You're not hurt, are you?"

I shake my head no and continue, "The men who attacked you were Russian, or Eastern European. Does that mean anything to you?"

"Russian? Why should that mean anything to me?" Abassi's cheeks flush and his heart monitor picks up a bit of speed. He glances at the guard. "Roland, some water please. It's terribly warm in here." The guard looks up from his magazine with a stony expression. He stands up, walks over to the other guard, whispers in his ear, and assumes the post outside the door. His underling goes off in search of water.

I lower my voice and say as sweetly as possible, "Look, Mr. Abassi, a man tried to kill me. His partner almost killed you." I hope this reminds him—without Max and me, he might not be here. Then I look him directly in the eye. "I need to know where that briefcase was going. Who was the intended recipient?"

A shadow crosses Adar Abassi's eyes. He glances at Roland. Is he wondering about his water? Or checking to see if the other guard is within earshot?

"I've made that same delivery, periodically, for several years," he says in a low voice. "I fly to The Kingdom and someone meets me at the airport. A courier, like me. But I have no idea what is in the briefcase or who the eventual recipient is meant to be."

"Is it the same courier each time?"

"Yes."

"Do you know him?"

"I do, but not *socially*. His name is Ali Kabir. He signs for the case." There's a tone of disdain in Abassi's voice as he emphasizes the word socially.

The second guard returns with a crystal pitcher of water. He fills a glass on the bedside table and then sets the pitcher down. There's a tension that causes me, instinctively, to wait before asking any more questions. Abassi nods and the guards resume their original posts.

"Why not socially?"

"Ali Kabir is Bedouin." There it is again. The sidelong glance at

Roland, who seems to have settled back into his magazine but is undoubtedly aware of everything in the room. I look at Evan for clarification. What difference does being Bedouin make?

"Desert dwellers," Evan says simply.

I wait for more explanation. He continues, "In Saudi Arabia, the Bedouin are considered by some to be backwards. Set in old ways. They don't really... mix."

Struggling to be politically correct is causing Evan to come off not just privileged, but obtuse.

"So they're like second-class citizens? Service people?" I can't resist. Evan cringes and struggles for an answer.

"No. Just old fashioned. Slow to adapt. There is a long-standing bias against the Bedouins. Many of the Saudi elite, including Mohammad, feel the Bedouin way of life has been trampled by modernization. In fact, Mohammad tries to find ways to accommodate them. He makes an effort to hire Bedouins whenever possible and encourages others to do so. He feels these acts of inclusion will heal and unite The Kingdom."

"You don't like Bedouins, Mr. Abassi?"

"Not particularly," he replies dismissively.

"Come now, Adar." Evan scolds. "Their wisdom, dress, and customs are the heart of The Kingdom."

As fascinating as this is, I'm not interested in a social debate.

"So the sheik knows Ali Kabir?"

They laugh in unison. Evan explains, "Mohammad's company, Bokra International, is a multi-billion-dollar business, Jenna. That's like asking if the CEO of ExxonMobil knows every person who pumps gas."

"Does Bokra International have ties to Russia?"

I'm hoping to catch another reaction from Abassi, but he remains poker faced, while Evan jumps in to answer, "It's very possible. Bokra is an international company."

There's a knock at the door, and a uniformed attendant enters with a rolling cart. Like a fancy hotel meal, Abassi's lunch is served under a silver dome. There's a place setting with a cloth napkin and a single creamy white rose standing in a cut crystal bud vase. Roland inspects it before allowing the attendant to set up the tray.

"Rack of lamb, fresh asparagus, and fingerling potatoes with truffle oil, sir." The attendant lifts the lid quickly to show off the plate and then covers it to keep in the heat. Damn, that looks good.

"Can I get anything for your guests?" he asks, rolling the cart within Abassi's easy reach before locking the wheels.

"No, we're just leaving, thank you." Evan nods to the attendant, then says to Abassi, "Feel better Adar. And again, thank you, my friend." Evan leans over and gives Adar as much of a man hug as possible while remaining wary of the bandages and wires.

"Miss Stack?" Abassi gestures for me to come closer.

"Yes?"

Suddenly he seems older, more frail. "I really am very sorry you became involved." He removes the rose from its vase and hands it to me. "This is a Madame Alfred Carriere, an old breed. The scent is extraordinary." He wraps his hand around mine. As I take the flower, he holds my eyes with his gaze.

"Please don't think terribly of me."

Something in his voice gives me a chill. "Of course not." I take the flower and breathe in the thick, sweet scent. "Thank you." Roland looks up from his magazine as we retreat, leaving Abassi to his lunch. Our footsteps are loud on the polished floor as we cross to the elevator. "Wow. I feel like I just stepped out of a film noir. Is he always so formal?"

"Adar is just from a different culture, Jenna. It's hard for outsiders to understand. He's a good man. Loyal. Honorable."

Evan seems distant, only half paying attention. Did something register in there that he's not telling me?

That whole scene was strange. From the fancy room to the guards to the talk of The Kingdom and Bedouins. We came here for answers, but I just have more questions.

"Is there any way to find out more about Ali Kabir?" I ask. The elevator dings open and we step inside, the only passengers. Evan presses the "lobby" button. "I could stop by the office, see what I can dig up?"

"Good. Whatever you can find would help. Right now, Kabir is our only lead."

As we reach the ground floor, I check the time on my phone. "Oh no! Wolfson is going to kill me!" I bolt for the door across the lobby. "I've got to run. Call if you need me. Or if you find anything out."

"Jenna?"

I turn to look back. There's a wistful look on Evan's face.

"Stay safe."

Chapter 10
Criminology 101

A wiry, balding man, Professor Wolfson shuffles a deck of cards at the front of the classroom as I slip through the back door ten minutes late.

Wolfson is shorter than average, but with an air of authority that makes him seem taller. In his late fifties, he's partial to rumpled corduroy jackets and is full of intensity. He paces at the front of the room like a shark that can't stop moving. He riffles the cards as he looks out at his students. Is this the infamous card trick Detective Denning mentioned?

The classroom is one of those auditorium style set ups. I manage to get halfway down the aisle and find a seat without drawing attention to myself. But as I put my backpack on the floor and try to slide silently onto a seat, my chair squeaks loudly.

"Miss Stack. You force me to resort to clichés. So nice of you to join us."

"Sorry Professor!" I sit down with a thump. Wolfson glares at me for what feels like forever until the whole class is squirming.

"I will continue—" He steps up to a tall table covered with a black cloth. "Never assume that what you see is real until you have proof. And even then, continue to question."

He lays down three cards face up. One is the Queen of Hearts. "Keep your eye on the lady," he calls out in an exaggerated imitation of a street hustler. He picks the cards up, shuffles them around quickly, then lays all three on the table face down. "Sam, tell me, where is the lady?"

Sam, a nerdy CSI enthusiast, stands up tentatively. He's tall, slightly built, and always wears a baseball cap backwards, I suspect to hide premature balding. Today's cap features a New York Fire Department insignia. Sam takes a moment to consider his answer.

"In the middle, Professor?"

Wolfson turns the card over to reveal an Ace.

"How about you, Cody? I'll go easy on you and leave the cards where they are. You have a fifty-fifty chance of deducing correctly."

Cody is a jockish gentle giant in his early twenties who was a football star in high school. Now he wonders why his life sucks. He seems startled to be called on.

"The one on the right?"

"Your right, or my right?"

"Mine?" Cody replies without confidence.

Wolfson flips over the card. A Jack. He directs his attention toward me. "Jenna, would you care to make the final guess? I'd say your chances are excellent." Laughter rumbles through the classroom. I've seen this card scam on the street. I'm not sure how it works, but they never give the mark three guesses. This has to be a trick.

"Well, Professor, there's only one card left, which is a little too obvious and not to your point. So my guess is—the Queen isn't on the table at all."

I get a rare smile from Wolfson. Pleased with himself, he produces the Queen. "Excellent, dear. I *palmed* it, as they say."

I feel a rush of pride. Although if he'd called on me first, or even second, I probably would've fallen into the same trap as Sam and Cody.

"However," he continues, "this does not make up for your tardiness. Stay after class. I'd like a word with you."

Oh no! Wolfson has never asked me to stay late. The idea is less than appealing. Yes, he's brilliant, and he's worked for the FBI and the CIA. But there's something off about the guy. I mean, really? Three-card Monte as a teaching technique? I suffer through the rest of class in anticipation, watching the big industrial clock over Wolfson tick away the minutes.

To the right of the clock is a handwritten sign with Wolfson's Golden Rules:

1. Slow and Steady Solves the Case: Unless lives are in imminent danger, take your time. Be smart. Find the proof.
2. Trust No One: Consider the Source. Listen to all leads. Always be wary of secondhand information and biased sources.
3. The Truth is in the Details: No clue is too small. Trust your instincts. Follow up on all leads.
4. Always Be Prepared: You never know what might come in handy. Memorize, pack, restock, plan. A prepared investigator is a successful investigator.
5. Eat When You Can: If an investigation heats up, you might not have time to stop again soon.

As I'm pondering the brilliance of rule number five, Wolfson writes on the chalkboard in his slanted scrawl *The Seven Signs of*

Terrorist Activity and with limited explanation announces to the class, "Just for fun this week. Look them up and see if you spot any." I jot this latest "fun" oddity down and gather my stuff as the room clears out. With the class empty and no excuse left for stalling, I head up to the front. I missed that stupid test in first period, due to being hunted down by a psychotic criminal in Central Park. I'll have to make that up. I'm determined to preempt a lengthy interaction by throwing myself at his mercy.

"I'm so sorry, Professor Wolfson. I know I was supposed to take that test this morning..."

"What is going on, Miss Stack?"

"Pardon me?" I'm confused.

"With you!" he raises his voice. "You're exhausted, distracted, and now you're late. I thought you were serious about this class and this program. For someone with a natural talent, I find your lack of commitment quite insulting!"

Wolfson meets my eyes with his hawk-like gaze. I have been late a few times without any excuse other than poor planning. But today I have a pretty good reason. I see two choices. I can apologize and pull it together, or tell him the truth about the last twenty-four hours. It might gain me a reprieve and he might have some insight.

"Well Professor, the truth is..."

He leans in, staring into my eyes, perfectly still, a snake waiting for its prey to inch closer. Or maybe a teacher waiting for his student to lie poorly.

"I have a situation on my hands."

He leans back, lets out a deep sigh, and shakes his head. "Are you really going to neglect your education because of boy trouble?"

The deterioration of my relationship with Liam *is* one of the reasons I've been distracted, but I'm not going to admit that to Wolfson.

"No, Professor. It's nothing like that. Something happened. More like a mystery."

"A mystery?" He leans in again. "Do tell."

I begin with meeting Evan Blake, then go through the events chronologically. Wolfson sits patiently, nodding encouragement but not interrupting. When I tell him about the mugging and that I shot a gun, he doesn't flinch. When I mention the $100,000 hidden in the lining of the case, he wrinkles his forehead slightly. When I finish my story, he hands me a piece of paper and a pencil.

"Draw the tattoos, please."

I sketch the tattoos with arrows pointing to body parts. Wolfson looks over my drawing, then folds the paper and tucks it in his jacket pocket and continues to listen.

When I've run out of story, he waits a beat, then parts his thin lips in a broad smile, revealing crooked yellow teeth.

"My, my, that's the kind of trouble I'll accept as an excuse." Wolfson rubs his thin hands together vigorously and licks his lips as if he's about to devour a spectacular meal. He quickly pulls two chairs from the side of the room and gestures for me to sit down.

Mystified, I sink into one of the chairs.

"Now, we have much to discuss." Wolfson stares at me, his black eyes gleaming excitedly. "This is your moment, Jenna."

"My moment?"

He nods encouragingly.

"I'm sorry, Professor?"

"I knew you were dangerous. I could feel it. Like a magnet for trouble. You've attracted this *mystery*. The puzzle is yours to solve. It's your first case." He stares off dreamily. "I'm almost jealous."

"Mine to solve? Why me?" Not that I'm a fan of the authorities, but I'm pretty sure they're better equipped to deal with this than I am.

"Who knows why. We don't decide these things. But you've been selected. Perhaps a little earlier than I might have anticipated. But the case has come to you because it's time."

Time? For what? This is ridiculous. Is he going to bust out red and blue Matrix pills next? Sprout ears like Yoda?

"You don't think I should just leave this whole thing alone, Professor? Let the police handle it?"

He shakes his head disapprovingly. "Oh Jenna, for whatever reason, you've been marked. Isn't it really *your* job to keep yourself alive?"

He does have a point there. If I don't do it, who will?

"And what have I always told you about the police? They're resources, nothing more. Depend on them, and you'll end up in the morgue. Rule number four states—Be prepared. Someone is after you. Don't sit around like a victim. Use your skills." He taps the side of his head. "Use your knowledge of the field."

"Theory is one thing, Professor, but this is real life. A life I'd like to hold onto."

"It's okay, Jenna." He touches my arm with his cold, dry hand. "You're not alone."

I'm not completely convinced of that fact. "Where do I begin?"

"With what you've observed, of course. Don't try to make sense of it yet. Just tell me what seemed out of place."

I close my eyes and start picking through the last two days. "For one thing, they were *not* ordinary muggers."

"What makes you say that?"

"The way they followed and ambushed Evan and Abassi. It wasn't random."

"And—?" he encourages.

"And the one who followed me, Dimitri Solonik, he was

tracking me. Common muggers don't usually go around killing witnesses, do they?"

"Why would he want to kill you?" Wolfson drums his fingers lightly on the desk.

"Because I'm a threat?"

"*Exactly.* You need to find out who benefits from your death. From any of this."

"When I interviewed Abassi, he seemed nervous."

"Has it occurred to you Evan Blake and Adar Abassi may have staged the robbery?"

"I thought of that. But I don't think so. At least Evan seems innocent."

"Only the legal system presumes innocence. Rule number two —Beware who you trust."

"If Evan was guilty, he probably would have tried to kill me last night."

Wolfson nods. "In the future, I recommend you don't test your theories by spending the night with a suspect."

"I did have a gun."

"Fair enough."

I think back to the mugging. Max lunging and barking. The look of surprise on Dimitri Solonik's face once I got the gun. The way the guy with the baseball cap shot at Abassi.

"It's like they were thrown off. Improvising."

"You were a wild card Jenna, not supposed to be there."

"Maybe Evan and Abassi were never meant to walk away. Maybe those men were there to kill them and that's what I interrupted. Maybe the mugging was cover for..." I can't believe I'm saying this. "A hit."

"Bravo!" Wolfson claps with delight. "Now you're thinking like a detective." He pulls a strange device I've never seen before from his jacket pocket. It looks like a thin sheet of black glass, barely bigger than a business card. He taps the surface with his finger and a screen lights up. He scrolls, operating a touch pad, and then hands it to me. "Type your number into my phone, please."

I enter my number.

"I've never seen one like this. It's so small and light."

"It's a prototype."

I hand back the futuristic phone. I wonder what else it does— shoot laser beams?

"I'm going to do two things for you. First, I'm going to put you in touch with Nadir Rashid. I want you to contact him as soon as possible and use my name. He's studying computer forensics and is an expert on the Saudi Royal family, of which Sheik Ab El Malik is a member. Rashid also might be able to track down information on this Ali Kabir."

Wolfson taps the screen of his phone. I hear mine beep as he forwards me Nadir's information. "Second, I'm going to set up a meeting with a Russian colleague of mine. He may have some insight. In the meantime, remain alert. Those from either end of society, the inhabitants of the underworld and the rulers of the elite, have more in common than you know, Jenna. Beware of them equally."

I'm wondering what that's supposed to mean when Wolfson stands up, gathers his playing cards, carefully secures them with a thick rubber band, and tosses them in a ratty leather satchel. I guess class is dismissed.

I pick up my own bag to leave.

"And one more thing, Miss Stack. You have that rare and useful Pandora instinct, the insatiable need to open the box. I recommend you listen carefully to whatever that instinct tells you."

Chapter 11
Cellos Straight Up

Cellos is what I would call a semi-dive. Not dirty. Not dangerous. But a far cry from fancy. There's live music seven nights a week and happy hour even on the weekends. But aside from the occasional fight or police raid checking IDs, most nights are pretty tame. There's a long bar, easily handled by two bartenders, one on a slow night. Six worn leatherette booths with scarred wooden tables line the north wall. The DJ booth is up front, and there's a kitchen and a larger room where bands play in the back.

Sharon and I are two hours into our shift. Tonight, a local band called *Alligator Sausage* is steaming up the place with a heavy dose of rockabilly. It's busy but not slammed. After the last couple of days, the rhythm of the bar feels good, normal. Between band sets, we pour shots and mix as many drinks as possible. Then the band plays the first power chords of their next set and sends the bulk of the crowd streaming back toward the stage.

Luckily, Sharon hasn't asked for her jacket back yet. I'm not quite sure how to explain what happened without worrying her. She's not just the manager around here. She's also the mother hen.

"Don't look now," Sharon announces loud enough for the whole bar to hear. "I just saw LM roll up and he has Little Miss Twenty-One in tow." She shakes her head disapprovingly. "I swear the older I get, the younger they do." Sharon's been very sensitive about her age since turning forty.

LM stands for "Loser Manchild" and is the code name Sharon came up with for Liam. I can only assume Little Miss Twenty-One is Roxy.

"That reminds me. He left a box of your stuff yesterday." She picks up a towel and starts drying glasses. "I was going to toss the whole thing to save you the humiliation, but I wasn't sure what was in there."

Sharon's from the Midwest. She has fresh-faced farmer's daughter looks, long blonde hair, often in braids, pale skin, rosy cheeks, and big cornflower blue eyes, all packaged in rock and roll attire and topped off with a tough, no-nonsense personality.

Tonight she's wearing knee-high, spike-heel boots over black leggings. A long, loose top shows off her ample cleavage, particularly when she leans over. She's a walking fantasy, and great behind the bar.

Thank goodness we pool tips.

Liam swaggers in with his arm draped over Roxy's shoulder. Even without the Hello Kitty dolls, and with her clothes on, I recognize her. She's surprisingly tiny, as in five-foot nothing, with impossibly narrow hips. Her enormous breasts could not possibly have grown naturally on her birdlike frame. She's crammed herself into a postage-stamp-sized minidress, fishnets, and what I can only describe as stripper shoes.

She's topped off her look with mis-matched oversized jewelry: bracelets, necklaces, and giant hoop earrings. If there's any justice in the universe, her glossy waist-length blonde hair is the result of hundreds of dollars' worth of extensions. Her face is inoffensive, although overly made up and plucked.

I start washing glasses to avoid eye contact.

Liam lets go of Roxy's hand and heads straight toward his buddies in the last booth. He either doesn't care or doesn't want to deal, leaving Roxy behind to fetch their drinks. Typical.

Sharon flanks my side. If Roxy wants to order, she'll have to approach us both.

"We don't *have* to serve her," Sharon whispers. "Ya know? No shirt, no shoes, no scruples, no service. Let's see what she does." She giggles. I envy Sharon. She's so much more at one with her inner bitch than I am. Roxy stands at the bar, fidgeting, as if uncertain what to do.

I can't take it. Too mean. And I don't want to start shit with her or Liam. She can have him. I grab a fresh bar towel, tuck it in my waistband, and walk over. "I'm guessing Jack and Coke for Liam. What are you having?"

Roxy smiles a big, shameless grin and answers, "Just a soda water for me, thanks."

I pour the drinks. Is she sober? Hard to believe with Liam's life-style. I set the drinks down in front of her. She hands me a twenty. I make her change, and she leaves the bills on the bar.

"You're Jenna, right?" Her voice is high-pitched, breathless, exactly what I imagined when reading her social media posts.

"Yep. And you, I presume, are Roxy," I respond as snidely as I know how.

She puts out her hand to shake. "Nice to meet you."

Surprised and unsure how to respond, instinct takes over. I shake her hand dumbly.

"I'm really sorry about the whole..." she tilts her head toward Liam. "Thing."

"Whatever, I'm better off." I brush her off, trying to recover. "I do miss the apartment though." Not that it was that great, but I'm not sure what to say, and any apartment would be better than none.

She nods enthusiastically. "It's great. And the plants are so nice. You have a real green thumb. I hope I can keep them alive. I promise I'll try."

Wow. She's already been to the apartment? Who am I kidding? She was probably coming around while I still lived there. And now she's taking ownership of my plants? This is bizarre and way too friendly. I remind myself that she is not my friend—although I do appreciate her commitment to the plants.

"Yeah. In retrospect, I wish I'd kicked him out instead of leaving."

"Oh! I'm super glad you didn't!" Her eyes widen and she puts her hand to her throat, as if she hadn't even thought of that terrible possibility.

Hmmm. She's either dumb, shameless, wracked with guilt, or a sick combination of all of the above. I bet he's already moved her in. Of course he has. He can't afford the rent alone.

"You sure you don't want something stronger?" I ask. Maybe she'll lose some of the happy if she catches a buzz.

"Nah. I gotta get to work soon…"

If she goes into a glowing description of her new performance art piece, I might punch her.

"I can't balance on these shoes if I've had too much to drink," she finishes.

Wait. What?

"Where do you work?" I ask hopefully.

"The Slap and Tickle uptown. Pays the bills while I get my career off the ground." She winks at me as if we're girlfriends in the same club—strip club, that is.

"But you're a performance artist, right?"

"That too. But what I really want to do... is windows. You know. Displays? I really think I have something special to bring to visual merchandising. It's my dream." With that, she looks down at her outfit as if she's living proof of her ability to put together a look. "Well, I guess I should bring this to Liam. It was really nice to meet you, Jenna. We should hang out sometime."

Wow! My brain can't even catch up with everything that just happened. That was not the angsty, tortured artist I was expecting. I even kind of loved her colossal, albeit misplaced, self-confidence. She's definitely a train wreck, in her own special way, and I do love a train wreck. Always makes me feel better about myself.

"Learn anything interesting?" Sharon asks snidely.

"Well," I stammer, "she's a stripper."

"Obviously."

"And I definitely miss the plants more than Liam."

Sharon shakes her head. "You should have kicked him out."

The bar has quieted down. There are fewer than a dozen customers left, all slowly finishing their last-call drinks. The kitchen is long closed. Sharon and I are busy cleaning up. Liam hasn't left his spot all night, but when his buddies walk out, he stumbles over to the bar. Sharon inches closer to me, within earshot.

"You saw I brought some of your stuff?" He slouches against the bar.

"Yup," I reply coldly.

"I put in some magazines for you to bring to Tyler."

"Thanks." That was thoughtful.

"You know, Jenna, I believe he's innocent too. I just... it's like all you have time for in your head is Tyler. It's messing up your life."

"He's my brother, Liam. He's in prison. It's messed up. You knew that when you met me."

"Yeah, but—"

"Are you actually trying to blame the demise of our relationship on the fact that I care about my brother?" I interrupt him. I do not want to have this conversation.

"No. That's not what I meant." Realizing he's on shaky ground, he switches topics to the only thing I'd rather talk about less. "So, you met Roxy?"

"Yup."

"She's actually pretty cool, Jenna."

He looks at me with anticipation as if he's waiting for approval. He's got to be kidding.

"I don't need to like her, Liam. Only you do."

He stops to consider that. "You're so smart. I really miss you."

"Maybe you just miss *smart*."

I can tell that was a good one because Sharon is beaming a proud smile as she walks out from behind the bar, past Liam, and out the door, undoubtedly to get Wally the bouncer.

Liam brushes a lock of hair back from his impossibly green eyes. "Don't be like that, Jenna," he pleads. "You're the one who left. I'd take you back in a heartbeat."

A year ago I probably would have fallen for that. I really did love Liam. I thought we'd always be together. But so much has happened. I feel like a different person, and him trying to manipulate me just makes me mad.

"Really, Liam? And what would we do with Roxy? Adopt her?"

"No." He sits down on a stool, resting his chin in his hand and forcing eye contact. "She'd be cool."

"No thanks, Liam." I look away, refusing to let him hypnotize me. "You two seem perfect together. I wouldn't want to break that up."

He nods as if considering the dilemma seriously, then counters with, "Well, she'll be working late. How about if you just come over for a while?"

My cheeks flush with anger. I'm formulating the rant to end all rants when Sharon returns with Wally, a former athlete with the kindest disposition you can possibly imagine, packed into a rock-solid six-foot, six-inch frame.

"Hey man," Wally says gently, putting Liam's right arm over his left shoulder. "Let's give Jenna some space. Get you in a cab. You can sleep it off." Liam squirms in protest, but he's no match for the much bigger man.

"Thanks, Wally!" Sharon and I call out in unison.

"Pleasure, ladies," he calls back as he whisks Liam outside like an overgrown kid dragging a teddy bear.

Chapter 12
Tyler Day

Today is Tyler day, and it's going to be a long one. I got up early to the sound of mewling cats, fed them, scooped litter boxes, and counted heads before organizing a care package for Tyler. On the way to the train, I have to meet Wolfson's contact, Nadir Rashid.

I lug my heavy backpack to a Starbucks in the West Village. I'm in line behind an urban hippie when a skinny kid in his late teens or early twenties slouches up behind me. He looks like he just rolled out of bed.

"Yo. You Jenna?"

This can't be Nadir. With a combination of thick horn rim glasses, pork pie hat, and low, low jeans, he's a computer nerd, college age hipster, wannabe gangster hybrid. And what's with the "yo"?

"Yes, I'm Jenna."

"Nadir Rashid. Call me Naughty."

I shake his limp, clammy hand. "I'd rather call you Nadir if you don't mind."

He shrugs like it's no difference to him. I have a feeling he gets that a lot.

"How do you know Wolfson?"

"I'm a sophomore. Computer Forensics. Done some projects with Wolfson. Last year we did this cool study, assigned a psychological score to criminals in a database using the Enneagram system. Predicted childhood traumas seventy percent of the time. It was something. Wolfson's the real deal."

I don't understand everything he's saying, but it sounds like Nadir is the real deal too. I send him to get a table and watch his rail-thin frame walk away. I wonder how on earth his pants stay up.

I order myself a plain coffee and Nadir a caramel latte. When I join him, he's texting a mile a minute one-handed on his phone.

"So," he dives right in, "Wolfson said you're looking for info on the fam?" He's still fiddling with his phone.

"The fam?" I stare at him, baffled.

"You know—family! The Ab El Maliks." He pronounces the name *Mah Leeeeeks*.

"Oh. Yes, I was wondering if you could tell me anything about them. I looked around online but didn't come up with much. Wolfson wasn't specific, but he mentioned the Ab El Maliks are members of the House of Saud?"

"A lack of specificity is one of Wolfson's things. Keeps the mystery aliiiiive."

"Excellent observation, Mr. Rashid!" I exclaim in my best Wolfson impression.

He smiles.

"Seriously. That was a good one."

He smiles bigger.

"So?" I prompt him.

"I'm one of them, man. A member of the Royal House of Saud."

"You're a prince?" I try not to sound shocked.

"Hell no. I wish! It's hard to explain—the naming thing is complicated. In Arabic, my name is Nadir ibn Rashid ibn Asad Al Farhan. I'm the son of Rashid who was the son of Asad."

I wait for more while he sips his drink.

"There's like fifteen thousand characters in the House of Saud, including yours truuuely." He removes his hat, revealing a wild mop of hair, and tips it at me. "In Arab society, women keep their family name, so it gets confusing."

I smile and nod to show I'm following.

"We're all related to one King Abdul Azia. That dude has twenty-two wives and something like thirty-seven official sons. Do the math. Lotsa relatives. You were asking about my uncle, Mohammad Ab El Malik. That dude owns Bokra International. Offices all over the world. Worth billlllllions."

"Are you worth billions?"

"Naw, more like millions. Pop's got four wives. I got seventeen bros. The green gets diluted. Watery. Ya know?" He shakes his head at the tragedy.

I take a sip of coffee, enjoying the insanity of the moment— me, broke Jenna Stack from upstate New York, sitting at a Starbucks in Manhattan, listening to a royal Saudi kid complain about his bros diluting his green while enjoying a beverage that I, incidentally, paid for.

"And your uncle? How many wives does he have?"

"Straight up underachiever." Nadir shakes his head sadly. "Law says, technically, four. And you can keep marrying and divorcing them as long as you keep it to four. Uncle's only got two so far. Fatima and Cintia."

"Yes, I met Cintia."

"Epic MILF, right?"

"She has kids?"

"Nah, what?" He looks at me like I've asked something completely out of context.

"You called her a MILF. The M stands for Mom."

"Really? I thought it meant hot old chick."

"I think that's a cougar."

"Ohhhh." Nadir grins, happy I've cleared up the details.

"How old do you think Cintia is?"

"I dunno. Like thirty?"

Good thing Sharon's not here. She'd deck this kid.

"Isn't Cintia kind of flashy for a sheik's wife?"

"Aw man, we got this whole crazy new breed." Nadir types into his phone and then sets it down in front of me. On the screen are dozens of photos of Cintia posing at galas and in magazines. She's all over the Internet, glamorous, cat-like, not the conservative sheik's wife I'd imagine at all.

"What do you mean, new breed?"

"Western educated. Front row at fashion week. Covers up in The Kingdom and peels it off here. She did get me passes to the Gucci show once. That was dope."

"What about Fatima?"

"She's number one. Never met her, but I hear she's icy."

"In what way?"

"Ya know. Number one. Has Uncle by the balls. Surrounded by psycho-pants."

"You mean sycophants?"

"Like I said. Psycho-pants."

I humor him with a smile. "And Bokra International? What does the company do?"

"Hotels, banks, textiles—and there's a lot of rumors— weapons, gold. Oh yeah! I almost forgot. Bokra's got a fleet of cargo planes. Supposedly smuggled a bunch of art out of Iraq during the Gulf War. Pretty cool."

I don't know if cool is the word I'd use. From Nadir's description, Bokra is into some shady stuff. "Are any of the rumors true?"

"I dunno. But Uncle Mohammad and Pops once took me to see a crazy army robot suit. They seemed chummy with those dudes."

"Army robot suit?"

"Like right out of *Terminator*. Blow you away." He makes a shooting gesture just to make sure I'm clear.

I sip my drink. Uncle Mohammad must be pretty damn chummy to have access to a facility that makes futuristic weapons.

"Why did they take you there?"

"Inspire my inner genius. I was really into robotics for a while."

"Really?

"Sure. Ya know how people tell you they're a full-on genius, and you're like—uh-huh, whatever? Well, I'm the real deal. Prodigy. Robotics, electronics, computers. High magician. Hacker extraordinaire."

I'm not sure how to respond. I was asking about the robotics, not his genius. I don't think anyone has ever *told me* they were a full-on genius before, but I nod anyway. Despite Nadir's lack of humility, I can see why Wolfson brought us together.

"Okay, genius. What about Ali Kabir?"

"Oh yeah. Didn't recognize the name, so I did some digging. You know he's a desert dude, right?"

"You mean Bedouin?"

He nods.

"So what's the big deal with Bedouins?" Maybe this kid can give me a better history lesson than Evan.

"All you need to know is they're whack, Jenna. Tribal nomads. Big warriors. They've got crazy sayings like 'A strong will controls a glorious destiny.' You know, whack."

"My understanding is many of them are acclimatizing to a more modern way of life." I try to sound informed.

"Some. But a lot of them still live in the wilderness. Crazy fuckers, if you ask me."

"Can you think of any reason your uncle would be sending money to Ali Kabir?"

"Nope. No reason. Dude's gotta just be a messenger for someone else, or a messenger for Uncle. Lots of rich dudes hire Bedouins. Word is they're crazy loyal. And they need the green."

This lines up with what Evan told me. "Would you mind looking into someone else for me?" I show him Dimitri Solonik's ID. "He may be Russian or Ukrainian. Just anything you can find out about this guy." I don't want to part with the ID, so I snap a photo with my phone and text it to Nadir. When his phone chimes, he checks to make sure the information is legible.

"Got it. How soon do you need this? I got midterms."

Figures. I've got my own personal computer hacker, but he has to schedule me in between tests. "No time limit. But the sooner the better."

"I can see if Dimitri here turns up in standard databases quick, but if you want me to hack The Man, that'll take longer."

"Uh, standard would be fine."

"Cool. Thanks for the jolt."

We walk out together and part at the corner. Nadir heads North up 7th Avenue and disappears into the crowd. I'm glad I didn't put off our meeting. Hopefully, he'll be able to dig up something while I'm gone. I'm definitely seeing the value of Nadir, even if I don't always understand what he's saying.

As I walk to the train station, I mentally prepare for the long ride to Eastmoor Correctional Facility. I hate going to that old, stony building, but I need to see Tyler and find a way to give him hope.

Chapter 13
Eastmoor Correctional Facility

The bus rattles down a long stretch of public highway badly in need of repair. Through the grimy window, dry grass stretches out on either side of the road. I've made this trip a dozen times, traveling by subway, train and then bus. I'll wait with a bunch of other people, mostly women and kids. I'll get a pat down as they search my package, then wait some more. Finally, more than three hours after I've left home, I'll get to see my little brother, in prison. It's awful.

I try not to dwell on Tyler's situation, but it's almost impossible. I'm five years older and I wonder if there's anything else I could have done. It's a pretty pathetic story. My dad, who in retrospect, might have been some sort of grifter, left when Tyler was seven and I was twelve. Mom, a public-school teacher, was a rock. She got us to school, made us do homework, and scraped together money for field trips and supplies. We were doing okay until she got sick. Even with her health insurance, the bills piled up. I was already a senior in high school by the time we had to move to the rough side of town. Mom eventually recovered, but it was too late for Tyler. When he was fourteen and I was in college, the trouble started.

I remember Mom always calling him the man of the house. I wish she hadn't done that. I think it put too much pressure on him. Experimenting with drugs and getting into fights led to arrests. But he wasn't a violent person, and I never believed for a minute he would have intentionally hurt anyone. Every fight he got into was defending himself or someone else. He was never aggressive, at least not before prison.

Tyler is serving twenty-five years for the second-degree murder of our high school football coach, Joe Vitner. On a fall evening, someone broke into the coach's house. There was a struggle, and he was bludgeoned to death with a bowling trophy. Forensic evidence put Tyler at the scene, and his alibi was shaky. A witness saw someone leaving the house and later identified Tyler in a lineup. The circumstantial evidence piled up. It looked pretty bad. Tyler admitted having been at the house earlier that day, but swore he wasn't involved.

And then there was Sheriff Wade Parker. The kids called him "Stockade Wade" because he would haul you in for nothing. Sheriff Parker didn't even consider that Tyler might be telling the truth. He never looked for other suspects, and he made sure sixteen-year-old Tyler was tried as an adult. Sheriff Parker was running for re-election and saw the swift resolution of the case as an opportunity to bolster his campaign.

The whole thing just ran right over us. Maybe if we'd had money for private lawyers or investigators, we could have gotten ahead of the case. But that's the justice system—screwed up. And now my brother sits in prison waiting on an appeal. I visit him every chance I get. Mom is in a prison of her own, stuck up in Bell River, with her neighbors whispering behind her back and judging. I had to get out of there. But I also had to stick close enough to be able to see them both.

Leaning my head against the window, I nod off to a recurring dream. I'm on the same road where Tyler swears he rode his motorcycle the night Coach Vitner was murdered, trying to find a witness. But this time I'm being chased by that thug, Solonik. I'm startled awake as we arrive at the isolated bus stop, a few hundred feet from the grim industrial-looking prison.

Dave could probably come up with a glamorous name for the visiting room wall color, like Urban Putty. But to me it just looks like sad dirty beige. The tables and chairs are mismatched hard plastic. I'm leafing through the *Vanity Fair* Dave gave me while I wait, feeling the weight of the gap between the lives in the magazine and the life I'm living.

Tyler shuffles in, looking rough in his dark green jumpsuit. His complexion is pasty, his dirty blond hair stringy with grease, his hazel eyes flat and dull. He slips into the chair, looking years older than the last time I saw him. He was always a scrawny kid, but I suddenly realize he's gotten bigger. Filling his time lifting weights has put some serious muscle on him. He's looking more and more like an inmate. And the increasing number of prison tattoos just adds to the picture. I see fresh blue ink on his hand but resist the urge to say anything. I don't want to fight.

"Hey J." His voice sounds raspy.

"Hey T. How are you doing?" I ask brightly.

He shrugs.

"I brought you a ton of stuff." I ignore his dark mood and try to stay positive. "Coffee, creamer, fruit, shampoo" —I can't help but glance at his unwashed hair— "powdered Gatorade, toothpaste, two cartons of cigarettes, and I put money in your account for a phone card. I didn't have time to get the shoes. But I'll bring them next visit."

The truth is that with the cost of cigarettes, I couldn't afford to get the shoes also, but I don't tell him that. Better he thinks I'm lazy than know I'm struggling.

"Oh yeah, and some magazines from Liam."

"Where is he?" he asks. Liam used to come with me sometimes to visit. He made out like it was a chivalrous thing. But I suspect he thought it was cool knowing someone in prison. And Tyler liked feeling like I had a boyfriend looking after me.

"He's with a stripper named Roxy. Sorry. A performance artist named Roxy," I reply flatly.

Tyler takes that in without expression.

"Bummer. He was cool."

I don't bother to contradict him.

"School?" he asks.

"Actually, that's good. I like it." I'm about to launch into an amusing anecdote about Wolfson when Tyler interrupts.

"I don't know why you waste your time, J. What are you going to do when it's over? Work for some government agency making crap money framing fuckups like me? You're better than that."

Clearly, he's been thinking a lot about this.

"I can't be a bartender all my life, Ty."

"At least it's honorable."

Now I'm getting mad. My brother has never been one to judge other people's choices, and he knows my interest in criminology started because of what happened to him. "Maybe I can do some good by helping people like us."

"You mean people like *me*."

"I don't want to talk about this, Tyler. You're being a dick." I really only call him Tyler to his face when I'm mad. Otherwise it's T or Ty.

"Fine," he broods. "You took time out of your busy schedule to come see me. What do you want to talk about?"

"Did you hear back from the prosecutor?"

"Yeah. I got a letter." He recites it from memory. "Dear Mr. Stack. The evidence you've requested responding to the motion for DNA testing has unfortunately been destroyed in a flood."

Now I understand his mood. Destroyed in a flood? I clench my fists in frustration.

"Oh Ty, I am so sorry—"

"I'm screwed, J."

"I'll think of something."

"Forget it. It's over."

"It's not over. This is just a setback—"

"The evidence was destroyed! Even my lawyer says we're at the end of the line."

"Look Ty, I've got some ideas. Don't give up hope."

The only idea I have involves Wolfson and is pretty farfetched, but I'm working on it. I hate knowing Tyler is stuck here feeling hopeless. I wish there was something I could do or say to take his mind off this place. Looking at his hands, I'm reminded of the tattoos I saw on Solonik and his buddy.

"Hey Ty, I could really use some help with something."

"Yeah right, from here?"

"Actually, you are the perfect person to help me." I explain the tattoos, where I saw them, and what I know so far. My story has the effect I hoped for. Tyler's expression changes, growing more focused.

"Can you find out what they mean, Ty?"

"What have you gotten yourself into, sis?" Tyler shakes his head, then pauses to think. "I know a Ukrainian kid called Taras.

Tough fucker. Served time in the gulag or whatever they call it over there. He's got a star tattoo. He says the points are for time served."

"Really? I heard it was rank."

"Not always, according to Taras."

I lean back in the plastic chair. Tyler's firsthand information could prove invaluable. Why didn't I think of this before?

He nods and offers, "Want me to ask him about the other stuff?"

"That would be great." I take a risk and add, "And as long as we're on the subject, maybe you could lay off the ink a little?" I gesture to his hand. "I get it. You're bored. And maybe the endorphins help remind you you're alive. And all the other inmates are doing it. But seriously T, even if it's only for me, try to keep it off your neck and hands. You're going to need a job when you get out of here."

His face drops, and I realize I've messed up.

He shakes his head solemnly. "I'm never getting out of here. I'm looking at two more *decades*. That's like fifty years on the outside... in a really bad neighborhood."

Darn it. I should have kept my mouth shut. I've ruined our visit. The guard approaches to take him back to his cell. We're out of time. I can't leave my little brother more hopeless than when I arrived. I grab his hand and squeeze it hard.

"Look Ty, I'm learning stuff every day. I met a cop named John Denning and—"

"A cop? Like those fuckers who stuck me in here in the first place?"

I ignore his outburst and push on, speed talking. "Wolfson said if I do well this semester, I'll get an internship. I was thinking, maybe I can do it in Bell River? We can review the case together, Ty. Go over every clue. I'll do the legwork, okay? I promise you. I will not leave you in here. You're innocent, and we'll find a way to get you out."

Tyler looks at me in desperation, like a man in a raging ocean hanging onto a piece of driftwood. "Okay, J. Okay." The guard pushes him along, and I watch him disappear through the door, into the belly of the beast.

When I retrieve my personal items, I check my phone and see I missed a text.

Nadir: *Solonik in system. Record overseas. Came into US via NYC 6 months ago. Visa expired. NV ID prob fake.*

Chapter 14
Buster Keaton

After three more hours of uncomfortable public transportation, punctuated by intense guilt, I'm emotionally and physically drained. I head straight for the sarcasm, safety, and snacks of Dave's place without even thinking. I'm just about to enter his building when a text arrives.

Dave: *Help a lover out? End the day with a quick gig?*

He answers the door barefoot in a terry-cloth robe and a stretchy headband holding his hair off his forehead. A tube of face mask is in one hand, a glass of white wine in the other.

"Ooh! That's what I call service." Dave steps aside, letting me inside his apartment.

"I was on my way over anyway."

"Rough one?"

I nod, emotionally exhausted.

He holds up the tube. "I was just about to partake in some refreshing pore maintenance. Join me?"

He's a lunatic. I love him. He's just what I need right now. "No, I think my pores are fine today."

"Wine, then?"

"That I'll take you up on."

Over wine and with his lips barely moving so as not to crack his mask, Dave fills me in on the gig with a new client. Apparently Matty Cooper is a celebrity landscape architect whose uber-green NoHo apartment was featured in *Better Homes and Gardens*. Usually when a client is high profile or the home promises to be spectacular, Dave does the first visit himself. The fact he's farming out Matty Cooper, combined with the face mask, can only mean one thing. Dave has a hot date.

"This could be the one, Jenna. I met him in line today at the Trader Joe's wine shop."

Dave disappears around the corner to wash off the mask and emerges in flat-front khakis and a fitted T-shirt. He is gorgeous and ready to go.

"I thought we were off men?"

"Oh, please! I was just showing solidarity!"

"What does Matty Cooper have? Dogs? Cats? Birds?"

"No dogs. All simple stuff. A quick in and out."

"I'm not going to find six cats, am I?" You can't blame a girl for being suspicious.

"Of course not! I've got some easy dingbat on that assignment," he jokes.

I'm suddenly aware I should tell him what happened with Evan Blake, but now doesn't seem like the time. He's so excited for his date. I don't want to bring him down with the attempted murder of one of his clients.

"Come on. I'll owe you. You name it."

I've had two glasses of wine, and even though I could use a nap before my shift at Cellos, I need the money.

"Fine. I'll do it." I'll collect later by asking him not to freak out when I tell him I shot a gun while on duty.

He hands me an assignment slip with an address. Then he gets back to fussing about his date, loading keys and phone into his pockets and brushing a stay lock of hair away from his forehead.

"You know I'd do it myself. I'm dying to see that apartment. But I've got a wine drinking hottie waiting at Lillie's. I'll text you the details." Dave kisses me on the cheek and he's out the door.

I wash my hands and grab an apple. Then I look at the address. High profile Matty Cooper's fabulous uber-green apartment is pretty close by, so I decide to walk. It's beautiful out and I'm in no rush. My phone rings and a robot voice asks if I want to accept a call from a correctional facility—it's Tyler.

"I'm so happy you called," I say. "Sorry about getting on your case today. I just worry."

"It's cool, J. I'm over it. But now I'm worried."

"What do you mean?"

"I talked to my buddy about the tats."

That was fast.

"Great! What did he say?"

"Not so great, J. Are you sure it was an epaulet you saw, like military braiding?"

"Yes, exactly."

His voice sounds weird. He's whispering into the phone. "It means he's with a gang called The Krov. They're connected to the Red Mafia. Mean, bad dudes. My buddy says like the meanest, the baddest, the worst."

My stomach sinks.

"You need to stay away from those people," he urges, still whispering.

"I'm trying!" I joke, in an effort to make light of the situation.

"Seriously Jenna, Taras said you only get a grim reaper after twenty kills. I can't believe I'm saying this, but if you see them again, just call that cop friend of yours."

"I will!" You know things are ugly when the Stack kids agree that calling a cop is the best option.

Deep in thought over this Russian Gang development, I make it all the way to Matty Cooper's unassuming brick building before I realize Dave hasn't texted instructions yet. His date must be going well.

The doorman is expecting me. I take the stairs to the third-floor apartment.

Dave wasn't kidding about the place being uber-green. Cooper's apartment is a shrine to sustainable materials. The first thing I see is what looks like a wall of lettuce. I slip off my shoes, afraid of tracking polluted New York City soot into this all-natural environment. I walk across the perfectly polished bamboo floors to inspect the lettuce. Turns out they're vines pressing against a massive glass wall. Interesting.

Hot from the walk, and upset by Ty's call, I head to the kitchen for some water and to see if maybe there are any instructions on the fridge. The state-of-the-art fridge is free of any magnets, instructions, or other unsightly clutter. But the filtered water inside is cold and delicious. Cast iron pans hang from the ceiling. There's even an herb garden next to a mortar and pestle. I could get used to this, provided someone else did the pestling. A buzzing in my pocket startles me. Finally, Dave's text arrives.

Dave: *1 of 3. The kids. Location, the roof. Food, in cabinet on roof.*

The kids? What's that supposed to mean?

Peace lilies line a modern stairway. I head up to the roof. A heavy glass door slides open with a hiss. Directly in front of me, surrounded by reeds, is a lovely pool of water, with rocks and a waterfall. As I step closer to the pool, I see koi fish below the surface. Ah. The "kids" are a school of koi.

I find the food and sit on the edge of the pool. A red koi penetrates the surface, kicking up spray. She rolls on her side and eyeballs my hand. I sprinkle food and watch her thrash, scooping the flakes up in big gulps. Some of the fish are ghostly white, others bright orange. An extra-large one skims the bottom, black and gold with long whiskers. They all look healthy, with clear eyes and perfectly rounded fins.

Something about watching fish eat is relaxing, and I want to savor the moment. I wonder how often Cooper goes out of town. I wouldn't mind a stint here, what with the filtered water, roof access, and pretty fish.

After a few minutes, my phone buzzes again. Okay. What's next.

Dave: *2. Gaston & Gigi. Location, master bedroom. Food, mini fridge. Socialized. Then Buster Keaton last...*

Socialized? Now Dave is just being silly. Is he drunk, or is he forwarding me the crazy texts Cooper sent him?

Once I find the master bedroom, I hesitate before entering. There's a series of clicks and whirs, followed by a deafening screech. Whoever, and whatever, Gaston and Gigi are, they definitely know I'm coming.

Inside the room is a large cage surrounded by a play area filled with brightly colored toys. Gaston and Gigi are a pair of spectacular rose-breasted cockatoos. One bird lengthens up and peers at me, spreading her crest. The other twirls on a branch and clambers across the cage to the gate using his beak and claws. In the fridge, I find a container of fresh seeds, veggies, grains, and fruit mixed with leaves. I scoop the mixture into cups and slowly open the gate.

Star Simonsen, my best friend growing up, had birds, or her family did. So I'm pretty comfortable. I coo and make clicking sounds. One cockatoo trills back. I decide it's Gaston.

I hook the cups on opposite sides of the cage and am about to remove my hand when Gaston scuttles up onto my arm, stares at me, and bobs his head a few times. Startled by his boldness, I calm my mind and slow my breath.

The saying that animals can sense fear and anxiety is true. I learned at the shelter to soothe anxious animals and calm aggressive ones by emptying my mind, or at least thinking calm, happy thoughts. Gaston is fascinated by the necklace I'm wearing, a tiny silver-colored heart. He bobs up, pushing at it with his beak.

"You like that?" I dangle the necklace in front of his glittering, black eyes. Gaston delicately plucks up the heart in his beak, crushes and drops it unceremoniously, then looks at me sideways. Wow. Did a bird really just break my heart? Good thing for Gaston I bought the necklace for five dollars at Old Navy. No big loss. Although it was pretty.

"Okay Gaston, you've made your point. Who's a big, tough bird." I carefully set him back in the cage next to Gigi, who is the more shy, and by extension more polite, of the two.

That just leaves Buster Keaton.

Dave: *Last One. Feed, mist, change water. Location, arboretum, up spiral staircase. Food, obvious.*

Obvious? I head back to the main part of the apartment and find a tight spiral staircase, hidden behind a large Ficus tree. I clamber up, navigating the twists and turns.

At the top of the landing, light pours down from a beautiful skylight into an indoor greenhouse. First a roof and now a plant-filled secret room? I'm liking this place more and more. I look around for Buster Keaton.

"Buster?" I feel pretty stupid. I don't even know what I'm looking for. A monkey? A pot-bellied pig?

Over in the corner, light glints off a cage full of little white mice. My first thought is CUTE! Then my stomach tightens when I notice the large glass wall next to the mice, a terrarium so well camouflaged, I didn't see the glass at first.

Inside, pieces of driftwood crisscross under glossy leaves. Then a mottled green and yellow striped pattern emerges—and the pattern moves.

A huge, maybe four-foot long, lizard looks at me through the glass, opens his mouth in a cat-like hiss, before swishing his tail with a thump. This must be Buster Keaton.

A tingle of fear runs down my legs and I actually think, for a split second, I may have peed myself. My knees weaken. Next to the lizard's habitat is the sacrificial cage. The mice are wiggling their pink noses and cleaning themselves, completely unaware they are food.

A wave of revulsion passes over me. I don't like snakes or lizards or anything with scales. I don't like feeding live things to other live things, and I don't like the possibility of being bitten by something that looks more like a dinosaur than a pet. I pull my phone out and text Dave.

Me: *Absolutely not.*
Dave: *Just this once?*
Me: *I do not like lizards and I will not sacrifice mammals under any circumstances!*
Dave: *Feeding pets is part of your new job description.*
Me: *No! It's cruel. And this thing is scary. I'll faint. I'll die.*

They'll find me here dead if it doesn't eat me first.
Dave: *Don't make me cut my date short! You're already there.*
Think danger pay!
Me: *I'll change the water and mist him. That's it. No mice.*
Dave: *Pleeeeaaase!!!*
Me: *NO! Lizard dinner = your problem.*

I'm here already, so I make sure Buster's hydration needs are met. But then I'm gone. I open the side of the terrarium. Clammy sweat trickles down my cheek.

The lizard shakes his head. He seems wary of me. Good. Hopefully he'll hang back and not confuse my fingers with food. I flush out his water pool and refill it. As I mist the air, he lashes his tail in a warning and hisses, showing me his formidable teeth. I freeze. My breath catches in my throat. I try to blank my mind, but it's not working. Come on, Jenna. Think about something nice. Butterflies and hummingbirds, unicorns and rainbows. Stop thinking about fluffy little mice squealing in horror as they are snapped in two.

Arrrgh! I lock the cage and back away.

I almost break my neck racing down the spiral staircase that can't possibly be up to code. I worry that I didn't latch the cage properly and Buster is on my tail when my phone buzzes. If Dave thinks he can get me back up those stairs, he's out of his mind. I don't care how well his date is going.

It's not Dave.

Wolfson: *Bar Kiev. Midtown. 7 p.m. Alone.*

Thank goodness. I could use a shot of vodka.

Chapter 15
Bar Kiev

Bar Kiev is a few steps down from street level. Behind a heavy lacquered door with beveled glass, the room is narrow but deep and very dark. The blackness is broken up with low hanging bulbs covered in red fringed lampshades, casting a strange demonic glow. It takes a minute for my eyes to adjust.

What a contrast from Matty Cooper's greentopia. From light and airy to dark and eerie. As long as there aren't any reptiles here, I'll be fine.

There's a heavily made-up, extremely beautiful brunette at the bar talking to a big, rough bartender. Also at the bar are some tourist types mixed in with businessmen. It's not looking very Russian to me, until I notice dozens of glass vats behind the bartender. Each one is filled with clear liquid, I assume vodka, and some sort of flavoring ingredient: rosemary sprigs, vanilla beans, pineapple rings.

There's no sign of Wolfson at the bar, so I walk deeper into the room, stumbling as I navigate the darkness. A wild roar, as if someone just scored a game-winning touchdown, bursts out from the darkness. I don't see any TVs. I push deeper into the room, scanning the tables and the few customers.

"Jenna!" Wolfson waves from the back of the room. I make my way over and find him sitting, arm in arm, with an older man. The pair wear wide smiles on their ferret-like faces. A bottle of vodka sits on the table between them—half full.

Wolfson's buddy stands up. Two gold teeth glitter in the low light. He's wiry, like Wolfson, but with heavy brows. When I look into his eyes, I'm shocked by a ragged scar running from his hairline, down through his left eyebrow and into his eyelid, causing the skin to pucker unnaturally. That must have hurt.

"Jenna, meet my dear friend—" Before Wolfson has a chance to finish, the other man interrupts. He pounds his chest lightly, winks his good eye, and whispers with a long S sound, "Ssssssergei. Sergei Harkov."

"Nice to meet you." I'm completely flustered. The rumor is Wolfson has a sketchy past. Of course, I know he has a life outside of class. I just never thought about the cast of characters inhabiting it.

Sergei and Wolfson each have what looks like a juice glass in front of them. There are extra glasses lined up. A few are turned upside down on the table.

Sergei slams back the rest of his drink, then turns his glass over. He fills a fresh glass, pours one for Wolfson, then me.

"Sit! Drink!" Sergei insists in a thick accent.

I accept, sit down, and nod politely. I quickly realize he doesn't plan to continue until I drink, so I take a sip. It's definitely vodka, but it tastes like it's been infused with ethanol. A thin sound of shock escapes my lips. This seems to satisfy him. A second sip burns my mouth and throat but takes the edge off any residual anxiety from the Buster Keaton showdown.

"Ze Volf tells me you have mystery vith Russians?" They smile at each other knowingly, as if all good mysteries involve Russians. And what's with Ze Volf? Old code name from Wolfson's CIA days or just a nickname?

"Yes, sir." Not knowing who this guy is or how to act, I just try to be respectful. "I ran into some trouble."

"You know, not all Russians bad. But some, very bad. Tell me vat happened." Sergei Harkov looks at me intently. He has the same unnerving focus as Wolfson.

"Two men with Russian accents mugged my friend, Evan Blake, and a Hawala courier named Adar Abassi. They shot Abassi over a briefcase with a hundred thousand dollars hidden in the lining. One of them tracked me and tried to kill me."

Sergei speaks slowly, counting each question off on a finger as he asks, "Vat you see? Vat they look like? Vat they say? Vy you there? Is this Evan Blake, into anything... not so good?"

I shake my head. "As far as I know, he's clean. Two men followed Evan and Abassi. It looked suspicious, so I pursued, that's all."

Wolfson interrupts, beaming proudly. "She spotted their surveillance. See? A natural!"

They both nod approvingly.

"Vat these two men look like?" Sergei asks.

I pull out my phone, find the picture of Solonik's ID, and pass it to Sergei. He frowns as he examines the photo.

"Never seen him. Must be new guy."

Wolfson taps the screen. "Something about him is familiar."

Sergei shrugs and answers, "Rough business. High turnover."

"Hand me the phone please," Wolfson says. His expression grows serious as he studies the face of Dimitri Solonik. He punches a few buttons, forwarding the picture to himself, then hands back my phone. "I need to check something. In the meantime, Miss Stack, will you tell Sergei what else you noticed?"

"They both had prison tattoos. Not from this country."

Wolfson starts speaking in fluent Russian. He pulls out the sketch I made after class and hands it to Sergei, who looks at the drawing. They down another drink and chatter back and forth in Russian. Then Sergei addresses me.

"Stars on hand from White Swan prison. Very bad prison. Terrorists, murderers. Did other man have scar here?" Sergei slices his throat with his finger.

I nod, remembering the thick scar.

"Shoulder tattoo means 'thief in law,' big man in prison. Not mugger for sure. Sounds like Sasha Kurgan. A friend of mine tried to cut his throat once. Sasha killed him vith bare hands. You are in big trouble. You know about Krov?"

"A little." Thanks to Tyler. "They're part of the Russian mafia?"

"Worst part. Weapons, assassinations, stolen art. How well you know this Evan Blake?"

"I'm his pet sitter."

"Pet sitter?" Sergei grins, pulls out a worn leather billfold, then opens it and pulls out a photograph of an unfortunate looking, wiry-haired little dog.

"This is Vera." He strokes the photo lovingly. "Named after most famous Russian silent film star. So beautiful!"

He pushes the photo toward me. The poor thing looks like she was drowned, then zapped back to life. She has one tooth protruding from her bottom gum. Her tongue hangs loosely from her mouth.

"She's adorable."

"My little *lapochka*." Sergei smiles fondly, then tucks the photo away. "Now, back to business. How you get that picture?" He points at my phone.

"He chased me and I... kind of... bonked him on the head and took his wallet."

"Associate of Sasha Kurgan chased you? You live and take wallet?" Sergei looks at Wolfson, who slowly nods.

"And gun," I add. Not to show off. Just making sure he has all of the facts.

"Ah." He turns to Wolfson, grinning. "She reminds me a little of first wife, no?"

I'm not sure if he means his first wife or Wolfson's, but I can tell it's a compliment. I can't help but feel a little proud.

He turns back to me. "You kill him?" he asks seriously.

"Of course not!"

"Mistake. These men very bad."

More and more I'm thinking maybe I should call Denning, then hole up with the cats until this all blows over.

"Should I call the police?"

They both shake their heads scowling like that's an insane suggestion. Wolfson leans in and whispers to Sergei. They go back and forth in Russian. I sip my vodka and wait.

"I tell you what," Sergei offers. "If Sasha is in New York, he's on job. I will ask around for you. You have business card for animal care?"

I don't know what Wolfson said to him, but I'm grateful. I have a feeling if anyone can get to the bottom of the Russian connection, it's this guy. I dig out one of the cards Dave gave me and a pen, then write my cell number on the back and hand the card to Sergei.

"I find out anything I call Wolfson. This is for Vera." He pockets the card. I start to stand, but Sergei gestures toward my unfinished drink. I sit back down and slam the rest of my vodka in one gulp, then turn the glass over. They nod approvingly.

"Thank you."

"Listen, Jenna Stack. You avoid these men. If you can't avoid, you kill. Understand?"

Wow. I was just going to call 911. Sergei doesn't mess around. I nod.

"You need gun?"

I shake my head.

"She has Solonik's!" Wolfson interjects, glassy eyed, giggling.

Sergei laughs. "No no, that gun no good. Maybe used to kill people already. Police check gun, you go to jail. Too much trouble. I make you deal, Jenna. You take care of my Vera sometime, I'll get you a gun no one can trace."

"Thanks, Mr. Harkov."

"Just like first wife. Smart girl!" He smiles. "And call me Sergei, yes?"

"Sergei, then." My bartending shift starts in fifteen minutes. Bolstered by their confidence, the hope of more information and a healthy pour of vodka, I stand up to leave. Before I can turn toward the door, Sergei's bony hand clasps mine.

"Listen, Jenna Stack. You are brave girl, but you are in deep trouble. You are problem for Krov. You figure out vy they chase you. Vy you target. Until you answer questions, you vill never be safe."

Chapter 16
Shift, Interrupted

By the time I get to Cellos, I'm thirty minutes late for my shift. Wally waves to me and holds the front door open with one big, burly arm.

"You look rough," he observes, all smiles.

"Tell me about it." I duck under his arm and inside. This day is never ending. I still have eight hours behind the bar.

Sharon spots me and rolls her eyes. I don't plan to tell her anything about what's going on. There's nothing she can do, and she'll only worry. Problem is, she's pretty astute, so I need to keep the fibbing to a minimum.

"Sorry, I'm late—I had a meeting with Wolfson."

"Ew! Alone? He's so creepy."

"Wolfson's more peculiar than creepy," I reassure her. "And he's a total genius. You know he worked with the CIA back in the day? He also works as a consultant for the FBI." I find talking about Wolfson's past strangely reassuring. The man is brilliant, and he's keeping an eye on me.

"Whatever you say. If you're learning something useful that

could save you from the Liams of the world and get you out of here" —she gestures grandly at the bar— "I approve."

"I'm learning a ton. He's pretty amazing. Great stories! The other day he told us about meeting Viktor Burakov."

"Who?"

"Viktor Burakov? The Russian detective who took down Chikitilo." That earns me nothing but a blank stare. "You know, the Russian serial killer suspected of killing fifty-six women and children? In the end, they tried him for fifty-two."

"Uh huh." Sharon slowly cleans a glass with her bar towel, ignoring me.

"What? Do you live under a rock? He used to take them out into the woods and—"

"STOP! Gross! I don't want to hear about serial killers," she protests. "How about that practice thing you do? Amuse me."

That practice thing is a little observation exercise Wolfson taught us. We always have a lull between happy hour and the first band of the night, so the bar is pretty empty. But I don't want to disappoint. I look around dramatically.

"AHA! I can tell the leering guy at the end of the bar either really wants a drink or really wants to bite you on the ass."

"Or both," she quips as she walks over to help him.

Sharon pours the guy a beer, then comes back over to me and whispers, "Seriously, show me what you've got. What's *his* story?" She points to a guy in ripped jeans with scruffy hair and an old Aerosmith T-shirt.

"Musician?" she speculates.

"Hmmm... Let's see..." I take a lap around the place, wiping tables so I can discreetly check him out. Then I circle back, rub my palms together and finalize my findings before launching into my report.

"Vintage T-shirt. Designer jeans. He's not broke."

"Could be thrift store," Sharon protests.

I counter, "If it's thrift store in this city, he's still not broke. And he has no noticeable calluses or other tell-tale signs of habitual rehearsal. So, probably not a musician."

"Or not a very good one," she interjects.

"Touché! He's here early, changed seats twice, like he's picking a good spot to be here a while. So I'm going to say he's with the band, but behind the scenes. Maybe a lawyer, or manager?"

"What about him personally?"

"Between the laugh lines and gray in his stubble, I'd say he's late thirties or forty-ish with a little bit of *help*." I mime shooting a hypodermic needle into my forehead, the universal symbol for Botox.

"No shame in that." Sharon isn't one to judge, particularly an age-appropriate man within charming distance.

And that's when I go in for the kill. "And you might find this interesting. Note the tan line on his fourth finger? That's where his wedding ring usually is—or used to be. So he's either a cheater or freshly single."

"Well, which one is it?"

I watch the target for another moment.

"A married hound would check out every woman in the place. Instead, this guy's kinda slumped over, staring into his beer. My guess is he's newly single." I stop to take a breath and consider if I've missed anything.

I've lost Sharon's attention. She's now giving this guy a serious once over. Then a scrawny guy in a tank top with disproportionate biceps walks up to our subject. They chat and money changes hands.

"So he *is* the money guy!" Sharon looks at me, impressed.

"I'm going to say manager. He just handed that drummer a twenty."

"Okay, let's see how right you are." Sharon walks over to Aerosmith-T and turns on the charm full throttle, while I tie on a bar apron and pour myself a Diet Coke.

A few minutes later, she comes back, her expression suitably stunned. "That gave me chills, Jenna. You nailed him. Plus you saved me research time."

I take a small bow and tip an imaginary hat to my own brilliance. Then I check my phone one last time before we get busy.

Evan: *Back to the office tomorrow. Walk Max? Please? Security in lobby can escort you.*

Evan Blake certainly blows hot and cold. One minute we're spooning, and now I'm back to being the dog walker. As much as I wish it didn't, my heart skips a beat. I would have preferred an *I miss you*, but at least he's concerned about my safety. I'm texting back to confirm when Sharon interrupts.

"Wow! What about him?" She points toward the door.

I look up to find the very handsome, very arrogant Detective Denning, sashaying across the bar like he owns the place. He's got a restless, dangerous energy and a determined look on his face.

"Oh, he's a cop," I reply dismissively while finishing up my text.

"How can you tell?"

Oops. That's right. I haven't told Sharon a thing about the mugging.

Denning sidles up to the bar. "Miss Stack."

"Detective Denning."

Sharon leans over the bar, accentuating her cleavage. "And I'm Sharon. Can I get you something?"

He meets her gaze, then looks slowly and obviously down to her cleavage, then back up and flashes a smile. "No thanks, hon."

Oooh. Denning has no idea who he's messing with. Calling Sharon hon is like poking a wounded bear. This should be fun. But rather than claw his face off, Sharon smiles back flirtatiously. "Just let me know if you change your mind."

What?!

"Will do," he flirts back and then turns to me. "Miss Stack?"

"*Please,* call me Jenna."

He ignores me.

"Miss Stack, I need to have a word with you."

I gesture to a bar stool.

"Not here." He nods toward the door.

I'm not going anywhere with this guy. I just got here. Besides, I want to hear back from Sergei before I spill the story of the last few days to anyone. I trust Wolfson's judgment.

"I can't leave."

"It's okay, J." Of course Sharon is eavesdropping. "We're not busy yet. Go ahead." She has no idea what's going on, but she knows I don't like cops. She's just trying to get on Denning's good side.

"No. Really. *I can't leave.*" I glare at Sharon, who gets the hint and walks to the other side of the bar.

I lean in. "Listen, Denning. I'm on thin ice with my boss here already. I can't just leave in the middle of my shift."

"I'm not eager to spend time with you either, Miss Stack. But I need you to come with me *now.* We can talk in my car just outside." He crosses his arms over his chest as if he's not going anywhere unless I join him.

Remembering his stamina the night he questioned me, I want to get this over with quickly.

"Fine, but just a minute." I signal to Sharon and follow him outside.

Wally nods as we walk out past him. I suspect Denning badged him on the way in because his undercover car is parked illegally at the curb. Once inside Denning's Dodge Charger, I turn to him.

"Okay. What's up?"

Rather than answering my question, he turns on the motor, glances in his side-view mirror, and points at my seat belt. "Buckle up."

"Wait! You didn't say anything about going anywhere."

He ignores me and pulls away from the curb.

"This is kidnapping!"

"Arrest me."

Chapter 17
A Covert Affair

Denning turns down a side street and pulls up behind a black van with opaque windows, parked beneath a broken streetlamp. This does not look good.

"You're not taking me to the station?"

"Never said I was." He stares straight ahead, jaw set. "Things have gotten a little more... complicated."

"Complicated?"

One of the doors on the back of the van opens slightly, like an invitation.

"Come on," Denning replies obtusely. "He's waiting."

Why did I leave the bar with this guy? Oh yeah, cuz he's a cop. What was I thinking?

"Who's waiting?"

Denning ignores me and steps out of the car, gesturing for me to follow. He leans against the back door of the van and mumbles something.

I unbuckle my seat belt and step out, trying to see past him into the dark interior. The hair on the back of my neck bristles. As I inch closer, I see the soft blue glow of electronic equipment.

A surveillance van?

Denning turns around and faces me. "I'll be in the car. Any problems, scream," he says, smiling.

"Very funny. What's going on?"

Instead of answering, he grasps my elbow and hoists me up into the van. I turn to look at him, and I see something in his eyes. He doesn't like this situation either.

"Seriously. I'm right outside." He shuts the door behind me with a loud thud. Other than the faint blue glow, it's pitch-black inside.

All I can make out is the outline of a man, sitting by a wall of equipment in a low chair. He's turned away, adjusting a dial. He motions me over. Denning's partner? Supervisor?

"Have a seat, Miss Stack." There's something strange about his accent. American but with an edge. Static fills the air with a buzzing white noise that grates my nerves.

As my eyes slowly adjust to the darkness, I gasp. There's an eight-pointed star tattoo on his right hand. He turns to face me, and a jolt of fear rushes through my gut.

There's a long gash across his left temple and a dark bruise on his cheek.

It's *Dimitri Solonik!*

I jump up, slamming my head against the ceiling, and make a break for the door. I don't know what's going on, but I'm not going to stick around and find out. Before I can get my fingers on the handle, his hand locks around my wrist. I'm about to scream for Denning when Solonik flips open a wallet with his free hand and shoves it toward me.

I stare at a familiar badge with a distinctive golden eagle—the same one I've seen a dozen times in textbooks and online. Wolfson's a stickler for making sure we can recognize fake badges, a standard ploy of con artists. In the dim light, I examine the badge for color and size. On the other side is an official identification card.

Special Agent Cole Braedon:
Federal Bureau of Investigation

"You've got to be kidding. You're a Fed?" I'm trying to process this development and what it means, disguising the horror in my voice, while noting the huge bruise on his face where I slammed him with the metal pipe.

He nods, still holding my wrist tightly.

"Can I have my hand back now?"

"Are you planning on hitting me again?"

"No."

"That's a relief." He lets go and rubs his jaw. "I've got a hairline fracture, thanks to you. I still might have you arrested for assault. I haven't decided yet."

"Assault? I thought you were going to kill me! Next time, maybe you should identify yourself. Why were you chasing me, anyway?"

"Believe it or not, I was making sure you were safe."

"By chasing me with a gun?"

"I'm working undercover—obviously. My associate was instructed to eliminate you. I offered to do the job myself so I could botch it. I had to make the chase look real, in case I was being watched. I could have shot and killed you several times. I was trying to catch up and warn you discreetly."

"Does Dimitri Solonik even exist?"

"Only on paper."

This explains why Sergei Harkov didn't recognize him.

I slowly sink down onto the floor, then lean back and wrap my arms around my knees. Could this week get any weirder?

Special Agent Braedon leans forward into the light cast by the electronic equipment. His wide-set eyes are a stormy green, not bright like Liam's, deeper, more guarded. His brow cuts straight across his forehead, giving him a solemn expression. His dark hair is longish and messy, his jaw defined but unshaven.

"Would you like some water?" he asks in a soft voice.

"Yes, please."

He uncaps a bottle of spring water. I take a sip and rest my head on my knees, feeling more than a little overwhelmed. Agent Braedon eases off the chair and leans back on the side of the van, so we're at eye level.

"I'm sorry you got pulled into this, Jenna. Can I call you Jenna?"

I shrug. "Sure, if I can call you Cole."

"Done."

"I thought you weren't allowed tattoos in the FBI."

"Not on your arms or hands." He points to the eight-pointed star on his hand. "This is fake. The real one was removed years ago." He pulls his shirt up. Across his ribs is an elaborate network of tattoos. "I'm still working on removing these." He smiles a sad smile. "Hurts like hell."

"Where did you get them?"

"Another life."

For a moment he looks vulnerable, not a hardened FBI man, just someone caught up in the crazy currents of life.

"So what exactly is your cover? You're supposed to be a hitman? Isn't that awkward?"

"I'm supposed to be a driver. And muscle. The hitman thing is a new development, meaning the situation is devolving. I don't have a lot of time, Jenna. I have to get out soon, before they figure out I'm *not* going to kill anyone. I brought you here because I need your help."

"But why is Sasha Kurgan after *me*?"

Cole looks at me curiously. "How do you know his name?"

"A Russian acquaintance ID'd him."

"Who?"

"Sergei Harkov."

"Harkov? He's still alive? Wolfson introduced you?"

"You know Wolfson?"

He grins. "I haven't seen him in a long time, but yes."

So that was why Wolfson thought he recognized Solonik. Was he connected to every unsavory character in New York City?

"How do you know the professor?"

"I can't tell you that. But Wolfson said I could trust you, so I'm going to share some information on a need-to-know basis."

"You talked to him about me? When?"

"About ten minutes ago. I told him we'd be meeting. He's quite fond of you."

"Why am I here, exactly?"

"The FBI is investigating a Russian gang."

"The Krov."

Cole responds with an incredulous stare.

"Yes. They traffic in weapons. Sometimes they work as hitmen."

So, the mugging was really a hit?

"Why would the Krov want to kill Evan and Abassi?"

"That's what I'm trying to figure out." His eyes meet mine with a steady intensity. "I've been trying to find out who ordered the hit.

We know Evan Blake passes money to Adar Abassi regularly. Abassi then flies to Saudi Arabia and passes it to another man."

"Ali Kabir."

He looks stunned this time, an expression I doubt he's accustomed to wearing. "You know about Ali Kabir too?"

I shrug and sip my water. "I interviewed Abassi in the hospital."

"Listen Jenna, I need Blake's computer files. We need to know who's ordering the money drops in the first place and search for a connection to Ali Kabir." Braedon hands me what looks like a thumb drive.

"Just stick this in Blake's computer," he says. "When the light blinks, it's finished uploading the files to our server."

"Don't you need Evan's password for this to work?"

"We've got it."

I'm sure they do. For all I know, the FBI has people at the Genius Bar. Is nothing sacred? "Isn't that unconstitutional?"

"Not in this case. I have a warrant. Besides, wouldn't you like to find out who's trying to kill your boyfriend?"

"Evan isn't my boyfriend."

"You seemed cozy the other night."

He's been watching me? Yuck. I wonder how closely.

"And it's a chance to make Wolfson proud. He bragged about you. Said your curiosity is insatiable. Isn't that true?"

"Metaphorically speaking, yes."

"We can help each other."

"I don't need your help, Cole. I found out about Sasha Kurgan, Ali Kabir, and the Krov all on my own. I have my own resources."

"Okay." He leans back, releasing my gaze. "Let's say *you* don't need my help. Your brother Tyler does."

When I hear Tyler's name, a white-hot flare of anger rises up. Is this a threat?

"What about him?"

"You know, Jenna, if you're going into this business, you really can't afford to have a weakness. Anger can be used against you."

"Don't mess with me. What do you know?"

"That Tyler Stack is rotting away in prison for a crime he didn't commit. And I could find out a lot more if I cared to."

Cole stares at me in the darkness. He's got me and he knows it. There is nothing I wouldn't do for my brother.

"You're lying."

"Am I? How long did they give him? Twenty-five years? That's the crime, Jenna. I'm on the inside of law enforcement. You're on the outside. I can help you get Tyler out sooner, maybe even prove his innocence. But there's a price."

"And that is?"

"Evan Blake's computer files."

"That's it?"

"Yes. Simple. You help me, and I'll help you."

I flash on Dave telling me how simple the Matty Cooper gig was going to be. I have that same doubting feeling. Like I'm being roped into something I'm going to regret. But if there's any chance he's telling the truth, that he can help Tyler, I have to take it.

I snatch the drive from Cole's hand. "How long will it take to upload or whatever?"

"Not more than five or ten minutes." He grins like the devil, pleased I've accepted his deal. "Then your part is done."

Somehow, I doubt that. "Can I go?"

"You were always free to go, Jenna." He smiles innocently.

I step out of the van into the headlights of the Charger.

Denning leans out the window. "You okay?"

I climb in next to him and slam the door. He looks at me sheepishly. He knows he tricked me, and he knows I'm pissed.

I ignore him.

He shrugs. "Fine. Where to?"

"Where do you think? I'm actually working tonight, you know." I've been gone for a while. Sharon is going to kill me. As Denning cuts into traffic, I shoot off a text to Nadir Rashid.

Me: *Find out everything you can about Cole Braedon, FBI.*

Chapter 18
Inside Job

I did not follow Wolfson's rule number four. I am not prepared. I think Cole said the thumb drive would blink to signal when the computer upload is completed. But I don't exactly have his contact info, so I can't double check now. I suppose I could ask Wolfson or Denning for Cole's number, but I'm pretty sure I'm not supposed to just call the guy. I also didn't bring any props to explain a prolonged visit to Evan's apartment. I'm a mess.

I consider what I need to do. Should I log into Evan's computer before taking Max out? Then remove the drive once we get back? What if Evan comes home while we're out? Finally, I decide to violate Evan's privacy first and wait for the information to upload. Then I'll take Max out for his late morning walk. Might as well get the espionage over with first.

As I walk past Lloyd in the lobby, a large blond man in an expensive suit looks up from *The Wall Street Journal*.

"Miss Stack?" he asks in a Southern drawl. As he stands up, he looms over me, built like a mountain. I guess Bokra hires all types. At least I hope he's here from Bokra.

"Um, yes? But call me Jenna. Where are you from?" The thumb drive feels conspicuous in the front pocket of my jeans. Can he see the outline? Why did I have to wear such tight pants?

"Texas, ma'am. I'm Jerome, from Bokra. Would you like an escort?"

That's the last thing I want, but I don't want to seem too cavalier, so I pretend to consider his offer before responding, "No. I'm fine. Just going to play with Max a little, brush him, then take him out for a walk."

"Okay. Call down if you change your mind." He looks at his watch. "If I'm not here, it'll be Charles."

Ah. A shift change could work in my favor.

He goes back to reading his paper as I disappear into the elevator. Once inside the apartment, I greet Max and give him a treat to quiet him down. I check the apartment to make sure I'm alone, then settle in at the computer. Might as well get comfortable. Cole said the upload could take five or ten minutes.

I take out the thin, metal thumb drive. Am I really going to do this? Yes. Cole may have unorthodox methods, but he is an FBI agent. People could be in danger. Heck, I *am* in danger. And I don't owe Evan anything. I slide the drive into the correct port. The screen goes black for a second and then back to the desktop like nothing happened.

I guess that's good.

I can't help but think about the other night, Evan sneezing in a pink robe and cooking dinner in his boxers. He couldn't possibly be involved in anything sinister. Could he? He's a "glorified accountant" and a foodie, and aside from being a bit of a snob, a good guy. This is a violation of his privacy. I mean, what if Evan's tax returns aren't 100% on the up and up and this gets him in trouble? Wolfson always says listen to your gut. My gut is saying this is a mistake!

A bizarre web page finally loads, represented only by a string of numbers. The FBI is probably sucking the info out of Evan's computer right now. I just can't do this!

I yank out the thumb drive. The computer dings and an instant message window opens.

EB365: *What are you doing?*

Yikes! I jump up and slam the laptop shut. Can EB365 see me? Is EB365 Evan?

I grab Max's lead. I'm trying to clip it onto his collar as quickly as possible so I can leave, when I hear the whine of a hinge. I peek around the corner as the door creaks open.

A gun muzzle appears.

I back up toward the desk. Max looks at me and starts barking. I grab a massive marble paperweight off Evan's desk and coil my arm back, ready to throw it. I hold my breath, waiting.

An older gentleman, not much taller than me, with dark coloring and a neatly trimmed beard, enters the room holding a gun. Before I can hurl the paperweight, Max starts wagging his tail. Max knows the man. He's wearing an expensive silk suit, his fingers are manicured, and his tie clip is set with a large jewel. He's too old and too small to be one of the guards and too well dressed to be a member of the Krov, unless he's the leader—and why would he show up here? But he's got a gun and he's not amused, so I slowly put the paperweight down.

He sees me and narrows his eyes. "Who are you? What are you doing here?"

Luckily, I have a legitimate reason to be here, so I go with the truth. "I'm Jenna Stack. I'm the dog walker. Here for Max." I hold out the leash as if it's proof of my story.

"Oh dear!" His entire demeanor changes. He holsters the gun

so quickly I'm left wondering if I imagined it. "The young woman Evan told me about. Please forgive me, Miss Stack." He bows deeply at the waist, revealing a tiny bit of thinning hair at the top of his perfectly groomed head. "I am Mohammad Ab El Malik. Please accept my apology. There was no guard downstairs. I heard a noise. I was concerned for Evan's safety." His voice is low and sweet like molasses.

"Oh no. Of course!" is all I can think to say.

Of course you're the sheik, and of course you roll around town armed, busting into apartments surprising would-be hackers. If he'd been five minutes earlier, or if I'd decided to go through with Cole's plan, we might not be having this conversation. Instead, Texas Jerome would be hauling my ass to jail.

Suddenly, Max goes crazy, jumping up and whining. Evan appears at the door.

The sheik's face lights up with relief, and the two men embrace as if they haven't seen each other in years. I guess Evan wasn't kidding when he said they were like family. He kisses Mohammad on the forehead formally, and they clasp hands.

"*As-salaam 'alaykum*," Evan says.

"*Wa 'alaykum as-salaam*, you look well, son." The sheik smiles warmly and turns to me. "I'm afraid I may have scared your friend."

Evan looks at me, brow furrowed, but I wave it off. No big deal. I almost deserved it.

"This one isn't easy to scare," Evan says.

"Yes. The brave Miss Stack, who risked her life for my friends." I feel myself starting to blush.

"Come, Evan. I am eager to get home. We'll talk on the way." The sheik waves Evan toward the door.

Evan looks at me awkwardly. Does he have something to tell me? Or does he want me to leave?

"I was just taking Max out." I hold the leash out again like it's a hall pass.

The sheik beckons with his hand. "Come, come, Miss Stack. Won't you join us? Bring little Max, too."

I'm being invited along? This should be interesting. I tug on Max's leash, and he prances along with springy steps, making little snorting sounds, happy to be going on an adventure.

As I pass Evan, he plants a kiss on my cheek and whispers, "Nice to see you."

There's that familiar tingle!

Chapter 19
One More for Tea

I've never been in a limo before today. Riding in the sheik's white Rolls Royce is like floating uptown in a living room on wheels, complete with snacks, drinks, and a television. I'm not quite sure how I'm going to go back to the subway. I can't believe I thought taking a taxi was luxurious!

Maybe I can talk Dave into starting a limo business and use one as my home. As we glide through traffic, Evan and the sheik catch up on the events of the past few days.

"Have you had any luck tracing what happened?" the sheik asks.

"No. I've personally talked to every man and woman in the chain of custody. Everything is in order. No one knows how the money got into the briefcase lining."

"And you're sure the money was going to Ali Kabir?"

"Yes. But I have no idea why."

The sheik nods, then pats Evan's arm. "Keep trying. We've got to find out who is behind this. I am not in the habit of giving money to enemies."

Enemies? I thought the sheik was a friend to the Bedouins.

We pull up to the curb of an elegant old building with a curved edifice of red brick and stone. The arched windows have intricate iron balconies. Judging from the outside, all four stories must be stunning. What does a sheik's apartment look like?

Max barks happily and trots up the steps. We walk past two stone columns to a set of Venetian iron doors. I realize this place is *not* an apartment building, but a house. A house in Manhattan! How many millions of dollars does that cost? The sheik senses my amazement.

"Do you like the house, Miss Stack? It was built at the turn of the century. I like to think we are helping to preserve New York's history."

"It's beautiful." I try to sound casual, but as I look up at the carved stone, I'm overwhelmed.

A uniformed housekeeper opens the door. As we step inside, two armed guards bow to the sheik. Evan and Mohammad gesture for me to enter ahead of them.

The foyer is breathtaking: arched doorways, honey-toned woodwork, and tasteful antique pieces. A massive spray of fresh flowers is set on an ornate credenza.

Inside the door—framed in the soft light pouring through the windows—is Cintia. Standing next to her is another woman, also dark and beautiful.

"Jenna! How nice! We weren't expecting you." Cintia kisses me on both cheeks. I guess I've made it into the kissing club.

Just like our first meeting, Cintia is elegantly dressed, this time in a turquoise sheath with three-quarter length sleeves, flat silver ballet slippers, and silver hoops.

"May I present Fatima Ab El Malik?" Cintia gestures to the woman next to her, easily ten years her senior. Fatima has a leonine grace as she extends her hand. The sleeve of her long, multi-colored caftan flutters with the movement.

"What a pleasure, my dear." Her hair is black like Cintia's, but shoulder length. Her ebony eyes smolder. Her features are fine, angular, and perfect, her skin flawless. She has a chilly demeanor, but when she smiles, a genuine warmth fills the room.

The floor is so shiny, I can see my reflection. I feel embarrassed in my black T-shirt and jeans.

Fatima plucks Max up, allowing him to lick her perfectly made-up face, then calls out to the housekeeper, "One more for tea, please!"

Tea? For real? An hour ago, I almost got caught, and shot, hacking into Evan's computer. Now I've arrived in a limo to have tea at a mansion. I definitely made the right choice. I just wish I was better dressed.

Fatima leads us into the main gallery where a sweeping staircase faces a polished ballroom. This place is huge.

A flustered young blonde woman appears, carrying two plates. They look identical to me, but apparently there's a decision to be made. She shows the plates to Fatima, then Cintia. The women confer, inspecting the choices, feeling their weight, and then agree.

Dish drama handled, Fatima and Cintia whisk me into a small, old-fashioned elevator. Fatima hands Max to Cintia, then pushes the button for the third floor.

Cintia shifts Max awkwardly, holding him at a distance.

"You don't like animals?" I say, surprised.

"Oh no, Cintia is wonderful with all types of creatures," Fatima explains. "She's just not really a dog person."

Cintia offers a hand for Max to lick, which seems to assuage both Max and Fatima.

"Jenna should join us at the fête, don't you think? As a guest of the family? Adar won't be well enough. It's only fitting she take his seat at dinner." Cintia is asking permission of the older wife. I can see why Fatima has an icy reputation. She's obviously in charge, but she doesn't seem cold, just a little formal.

Fatima seems pleased with the younger woman's suggestion. "What a lovely idea. Of course."

The two look at me in anticipation.

"I'm sorry?"

"The fête," explains Cintia. "The Faux Fur and Furry Friends Fête."

WHAT? *The* social event of the season? And I've been invited not just for cocktails but dinner? Dave is going to D-I-E!

"Oh no, I couldn't. It's too generous."

I heard dinner tickets are something like $10,000 apiece. Even if that's a wild exaggeration, they're pricey. And what on earth would I wear?

"Don't be ridiculous. You saved Adar's life," Fatima argues sternly.

"And Evan's, too," Cintia adds.

"It would be our great honor," adds Fatima.

"And it's going to be fun," Cintia chimes in with a wicked smile.

"Yes, this is our big event of the year. Cintia has been working so hard assisting me with every detail."

The younger wife smiles at the compliment.

"It's going to be wonderful," Fatima adds. "We won't take no for an answer."

Cintia seems to really want me there. And I'm worried I'll insult Fatima if I decline. It would be a once in a lifetime experience. And I can hang out with Dave during cocktails. What the hell.

"I'd love to!" pops out of my mouth in a high-pitched squeal of delight that surprises us all, particularly me.

Max barks, and we all laugh as the elevator arrives at the third floor. We step out into an extravagant living room with an open floor plan, like a modern boutique hotel suite. I feel instantly at home. The decor is simple and direct, all dark wood and clean lines.

A low white couch is sprinkled with bright throw pillows, in what I would call yellow and orange, but the decorator probably referred to as saffron and tangerine. There are lush, healthy plants everywhere, making me wonder how mine are doing at the old apartment I shared with Liam.

To the left is a formal dining room with a large, walnut table, molded chairs, and a modern glass and steel light fixture. Next to the dining room is a small, beautifully appointed kitchen.

"Is this someone's apartment?" I'm a little confused about how this multiple-wife thing works.

"We all have our own space," Cintia explains. "This section of the third floor is mine. Fatima is right above me. The entire second floor is a mini Bokra International, which I don't love. So many strangers coming and going. But Mohammad travels so much, he likes to have an office in every home."

Every home? I wonder how many they have.

"I love it!" I gush. It really is exactly what I would do, if I had a "space," decorators, an indoor gardener, and a few million dollars.

"You do?" Cintia seems genuinely pleased by my approval.

"Oh yes!"

"She did the whole thing herself," Fatima chimes in.

Cintia blushes.

"Don't be modest, dear. You have a real talent."

"Mohammad thought I was being ridiculous," Cintia adds, "but it was so much fun! Would you like a tour?" she asks excitedly. Then she glances at Fatima, as if maybe she's gone too far.

"Go ahead." Fatima smiles. "Evan and Mohammad are

catching up. I'm going to take Max to play with Honey, and by the time we all get back here, tea will be served. Have fun."

Fatima brushes past the dining area, through an open arch and disappears into the hallway. This glimpse into their private lives has been fascinating. The two women behave more like sisters or best friends than competitors for the affection of a royal husband.

"Shall we?" Cintia gestures to the room. "I love an open floor plan."

"Oh yes. Me, too," I say as I follow her.

She points to the kitchen area. "But I'm not much of a cook."

"Me neither!" Another reason to like her.

We follow Fatima's path and find ourselves in a short hallway leading to a series of rooms.

The taupe walls are covered with family photos. I stop to look. Evan is included in many, as is Abassi, and several people I don't know. There are kids, snowy mountains, gorgeous beaches, people smiling on boats. There are even a few of Mohammad and Fatima, obviously from long before Cintia came along. She points to a photo of herself and Fatima in front of a fireplace, drinking what I imagine is hot chocolate in casual clothes. Fatima wears reading glasses. Cintia's hair is piled up in a messy bun. "Aspen. Last year. That's my favorite."

Cintia continues the tour, opening doors as we walk. There's a decadent bathroom, as big as any bedroom I've seen. Tiny glittering dark blue tiles cover the walls and floor. The centerpiece is an enormous bathtub with jacuzzi jets. She wrinkles her nose, embarrassed at the extravagance. Just as she's about to explain, I jump in to reassure her and we simultaneously blurt out, "I love a good bath!"

Next is Cintia's bedroom. A platform bed is made up with crisp white linens. There's a comfortable-looking chaise lounge in the corner with a worn blue throw and dozens of books stacked next to it on the floor. Many of the titles are on history and diplomacy.

The window looks out on a tree. Birds swarm around a bird feeder. The perfect bedroom. At the end of the hall is a door.

"Stairs," she explains.

That must be where Fatima went.

The last door in the hall leads to an office.

"Come in for a moment," she says, opening the door wider. What is it with home offices? They're always a mess. The curtains are drawn, leaving the room quite dark. A white couch and chairs face a desk piled high with a mix of fabric swatches, photos of flower arrangements, and menu samples. There are three boxes on the floor labeled: *Yes*, *No*, and *Maybe*.

A fourth box is overflowing with brochures and letters. I can deduce it's her method of sifting through solicitations from charities. I wonder if she does the initial screening before sending those that make the cut along to Fatima. On the wall to the right of the desk is an enormous seating chart full of stickers with names.

Cintia gets a fresh sticker from her desk, writes STACK, J. on it and replaces the one marked ABASSI, A. She crumbles up Abassi's sticker and tosses it in the trash.

"I'm so sorry Adar won't be able to join us. But we're so pleased to have *you*, my dear."

Cintia seems less and less like the spoiled princess I imagined, and more and more like a pretty cool lady. I still don't understand how her lifestyle works, but like Evan said, different cultures. Who am I to judge? And she obviously spends her time well. At least she's using her position to help others.

Cintia is now rooting around the desk looking for something.

"Here we go!" She presents me with a box, around six inches square, covered with white fake fur and tied with a gold bow. "Some people like to have a little souvenir."

I take the box, uncertain what to do with it.

"Go ahead," she encourages me.

I untie the bow and open the box. Inside is a beautiful invitation to the Faux Fur and Furry Friends Fête. Affixed to the invitation is a silver Tiffany heart engraved with the word *Awakened*. Written in calligraphy is a quote which matches a printed sign above her desk:

"Until one has loved an animal, a part of one's soul remains unawakened." —*Anatole France.*

"Our theme this year," she explains.

I hold up the pendant so it catches the light. A Tiffany heart? For *all* the guests of the ball?

"Does everyone get one of these?"

She smiles and winks. "Only very special people. Big supporters. The ones with lots of money who always come and buy a table. You know, that kind of thing."

I look at her confused. What makes me so special? After all, I'm only Evan's dog walker.

"But I have extras. And you *are* a special guest, someone who I believe understands the meaning of the quote. Keep it."

"Thank you." This is quite an upgrade from the tin heart Gaston broke yesterday! As I'm closing the box, I notice an alcove in the back corner, glowing with orange light.

Cintia sees me looking in that direction.

"Oh, come see." She leads me to the back corner of the room. I realize I'm approaching a giant terrarium, much larger than Buster Keaton's. "It used to be a walk-in closet," she explains proudly.

As I step closer, the closet is dark, and I narrow my eyes. Then Cintia flicks on a low, buttery light, and what I'm seeing becomes clear. Ice shoots through my veins and I stifle a gag.

Inside the space are several smaller terrariums and a collection of writhing, slithering snakes. There must be a dozen.

I stumble back, trying not to hyperventilate. Don't throw up in the nice jewelry-giving, party-inviting lady's office, Jenna.

Cintia follows me. "Are you all right? I thought you liked animals—"

"Oh. I do, I do. I'm just a little shy with... snakes." I shudder uncontrollably, giving away my revulsion.

"Oh Jenna. I'm so sorry. I'm a bit of an amateur herpetologist. I forget sometimes not everyone relates to reptiles." She glosses over the awkward situation brightly.

There goes my dream of being BFFs with a gorgeous, benevolent princess. I've insulted her, AND she plays with snakes.

"Yeah, I'm more of a dog person," I reply weakly.

Cintia shuts the door and takes me by the arm, leading me toward the dining room.

"Well, as Fatima said, I *like* all creatures, but I particularly *love* snakes. In my country, we have a myth about an ancient moon god named Wadd. Snakes were sacred to him."

"I see." I dab at my forehead where tiny beads of sweat have appeared.

"Here." She takes the box from me and opens it. She removes the Tiffany heart and fastens the clasp around my neck. I can feel the cool silver through my shirt. She takes my hand. "The word Wadd means love and friendship, to remain loyal. Now, let's eat."

Tea is everything I expected and more. Servants, tiny sandwiches, polite conversation. Cintia acts as the hostess, I guess because this is her apartment. She seats me next to Evan, who touches my knee twice in between bites.

Mohammad commands the room, telling amusing anecdotes about his most recent trip overseas. I try to remember all the little details so I can share them with Dave over wine later.

I hear my phone buzz but don't want to check it. Forget reality. Forget school and the bar and Liam and Cole. I'm with my new friends now! Okay, probably not my new friends, but at least I can enjoy this moment.

"May I call you Jenna?" the sheik asks.

"Yes, please do."

"You can't be planning a career as a pet sitter. What are your ambitions?"

Evan stiffens. He's embarrassed.

"I'm studying criminology at University of Manhattan, sir." Evan's reaction irritates me. I don't have anything to be ashamed of.

"My dear, would you do me the honor of using my given name? Call me Mohammad, so much more friendly than sir."

I nod. I'm blushing again.

"Criminology? What does that entail?" Fatima asks.

"Behavioral science, forensics, social anthropology, crime mapping, that sort of thing. It's really the study of the criminal mind."

"What a resilient and accomplished young woman you are," the sheik proclaims.

I think he actually means it. Fatima and Cintia nod in agreement. Take that Evan, you snob.

Fatima adds, "I so envy your generation. So independent. I got lucky with Mohammad." She looks at him lovingly and then back at me. "But what it must be like to be young and have so many choices!"

Cintia nods. Evan's shoulders relax.

I don't bother to mention those choices are drastically limited by a shortage of cash. Let them envy my "choices," like crashing on my friend's couch while struggling to make tuition.

The intercom buzzes. A somber Bokra International security guard enters. I notice the sheik discreetly checking his watch under the table.

"Sir, the group from DARPA has arrived early." He folds his hands and stands with his head slightly bowed.

I try to act cool but inside I am nerding out. The Defense Advanced Research Projects Agency? That DARPA?

Mohammad wipes his mouth with a white linen napkin. "Excuse me. I must get downstairs." He stands up.

"Shall I join you?" Evan asks.

"No. We won't need you until later. Why don't you see Jenna home and come back?"

Evan stands and pulls out my chair. I thank my hosts, and he escorts me to the elevator. Even with all of the fresh fruit tarts, invitations to furry fêtes, and Tiffany hearts, my fantasy world is shattered. All I can think about is DARPA.

"What business does the sheik have with the Department of Defense?" I ask Evan as we reach the ground floor.

"We have an active technical research department with a number of projects ongoing."

"What kind of projects? Weapons?"

"Oh Jenna, you should see the non-disclosures I've signed. But trust me, Mohammad is a humanitarian. Bokra is committed to developing non-violent solutions to the world's problems."

My cell phone buzzes. It's Nadir. He's texted three times in the last hour. "Excuse me—"

Nadir: *911. In person.*
Me: *What?*
Nadir: *You need to see this. Now. My place.*

Me: *On my way.*

Evan holds open the front door, and I step out of the fantasy world and back into reality.

"Listen, there's something I have to do…"

"Dog or cat?" Evan asks, smiling.

"Gerbils," I lie.

"Can I have the driver take you?"

"No, I'll be fine." As I head toward the subway, the cement under my feet feels a little harder than before I took that limo ride.

Chapter 20
Nadir Rashid, RA

My personal search engine lives in University of Manhattan student housing. As I walk in the front door, the smell of fresh paint and industrial carpet goes directly to my head. Breathing these fumes cannot be good for young minds. Then again, who knows what the undergrads are huffing these days? Paint and carpet are probably the least of their worries. The kid running the reception desk is too busy texting to look up. I breeze right past and into the elevator.

Nadir's floor is bustling. Several doors are open, music booms out of the rooms. Worry-free students are heading off to class with backpacks in tow, sitting at desks staring at computers, or lounging on beds texting. Nadir's room is at the end of the hall. Stuck to the door is a chalkboard that reads: *Nadir Rashid, RA. Can't figure it out for yourself? Knock.*

I knock.

Nadir answers the door in baggy jeans and a wrinkled T-shirt. His black hair is messy and unbrushed. His eyes are watery and bloodshot. "Hey."

"You okay?" He looks so rough, I'm a little concerned. Maybe he called me over to take him to see a doctor?

"Yeah, epic night last night. Epic." He shakes his head as he steps aside to let me in.

"I thought Muslims didn't drink?"

"Who says I was drinking?"

Nadir's room makes Dave's office look like military-compliant barracks. There are at least three computers and what looks like computer parts on every surface, along with clothes, food wrappers, empty energy drink bottles, and overflowing ashtrays. The smell is a combination of dirty clothes, junk food, and cigarettes, mixed with some other musky scent I can't quite place.

Nadir pushes aside a pile of clothes on what appears to be a spare bed.

Just as I'm about to sit down, something hairy darts out, hisses at me, and slithers under the bed.

"AAAAAAAAAAAAHHHHHHHHHHHH!" I scream at the top of my lungs.

"Chill, Jenna! You'll scare Raoul," Nadir scolds.

"What the fuck was that, and who the fuck is Raoul!?" I demand loudly.

"My ferret, Raoul. I'm not even supposed to have him here. Chill. Please?"

Now I feel bad. I didn't mean to scare Raoul.

"Sorry. He just caught me by surprise. You might want to let a girl know there's a ferret running loose."

Nadir ignores me, gets down on his hands and knees, peeks under the bed, and tries to coax Raoul out with baby talk.

"*Está bien*, little buddy. The nice lady didn't mean to scare you. Come on..."

Nadir has the patience of a ferret and, after about thirty seconds, gives up.

"Aw fuck it. He'll get over it in his own time. Just try not to be so loud. My head hurts."

"What was so important anyway?"

"Oh man, Jenna. You ready for this?"

I'm ready for anything at this point.

He glances around his room, sticks his head out the door and looks both ways in the hall, all with the exaggerated gestures of a silent movie villain. Who does he think is listening? Satisfied no one is lurking, he finally settles in.

"That FBI dude you asked me to check out, Cole Braedon?"

"Yeah?"

"He *died*. Ten years ago."

Huh?

"Are you sure you got the right guy?"

"I'm sure. On the surface, nothing too sketchy. But I dug deeper, and it got weird."

"Weirder than dead?" I furrow my brow in confusion.

"He's *Canadian*."

"Then he can't be an FBI agent. You have to be a U.S. citizen to join the Bureau."

"Exactly," Nadir says. "Something's whack for sure. I can keep digging—but maybe it's not the best idea."

No wonder Nadir is being so paranoid. The government hates hackers. Getting caught doing a background check on an FBI agent is one thing. Being the guy who uncovers something shady about an FBI agent? Or uncovers a fake FBI agent? Or someone posing as an FBI agent? That's a level of complication Nadir wouldn't want to risk.

"Okay. Don't worry about Braedon for now. I don't want you getting into trouble."

His face softens. He seems genuinely relieved.

"Anything else?" I ask hopefully.

"I did a little more research on the desert dude, Kabir. Turns out he's not just Bedouin. He's Zahar."

"What's Zahar?"

"They're the craziest of all those tribes. Used to be guards for my granddad, Faisal Ab El Malik, way back. Then some crazy shit went down. Now the fam and the Zahar are sworn enemies. Us and them."

That explains the sheik's reaction to the name Ali Kabir.

"What happened?"

"Dunno. But it must have been ugly. There's a full-on feud going. I asked around but no one will talk about it."

"Can you think of any reason your uncle would send money to Ali Kabir? Could Kabir be blackmailing him? Or someone else at Bokra?"

"Could be. The Kingdom is full of treachery and drama. Think of it like Shakespeare. You know, *King Lear* but with sand."

I hear a scrabbling sound. A lump travels under the sheets for a couple of feet, then Raoul pops his head up. He is gray and white with a little bandit mask over his face.

Nadir hands me his iPad.

"I made a folder with everything I've found so far. Check it out."

Nadir picks up a can of Ferret Bites and tosses a treat to Raoul, who munches on it happily.

I click through the information, scanning the text quickly. A name keeps coming up.

"Who's Hussein Khalid?"

"He was ruler of the Zahar back in the day when the rift happened."

"He's referred to as *Killer of the Firstborn Son*. What does that mean?"

"I don't know. That's all I've got so far."

"Okay, keep looking." Nothing else jumps out at me, so I hand the iPad back. "Can you find out if Kabir has any ties or legitimate business with Bokra? Or with Mohammad?"

"Whoa, Jenna! Don't call the sheik by his first name. Not cool. Not respectful."

"Oh no! It's cool. He told me I could."

"What?"

"I had tea with him today."

Nadir's jaw drops. "No way! How?"

"Long story."

"You find out anything good?"

"Not like this! You're amazing, Nadir."

He smiles proudly. "Well, I kinda made us an appointment, if you're into it."

"With who?"

"Dr. Ben Adir Sullieman. World's foremost authority on Bedouin culture. Old family friend. He's curated an exhibition at the Natural History Museum. There's a reception tonight and he'll be there."

"That's impressive. Are you sure he won't be too busy?"

"I already called and asked, he was cool." Nadir smiles. "Besides, he loves the sound of his own voice. And you're a chick —he's kind of notorious."

I let that one slide. "One last thing, Nadir. DARPA showed up at your uncle's today."

"DARPA? Are you serious?"

"Any idea why?"

"No idea." He shakes his head. "The sheik's into weird stuff. Robot suit, remember?"

The blankets rustle, then Raoul the ferret scampers over to sniff my hand, nose twitching. I stroke his head. I guess we're friends now.

"Oh, yeah. I almost forgot. I brought you a present." I pull the thumb drive out of my pocket and toss it to Nadir.

"What is it?"

"A real FBI program that searches out information and loads it to their server. EB365 might pop up and ask a few questions, so proxy yourself or whatever it is you do."

"Whoa! Awesome!" Nadir looks at me like it's Christmas and he just got a box full of motherboards. After agreeing to meet at the museum, I leave him happily playing with his new toy and head for the subway.

Keeping in mind rule number four, I have just enough time to race downtown, feed the cats, and prep for our conversation with Dr. Sullieman. Tonight, I'll need to dress for an opening.

Chapter 21
Weavers of the Desert

The Great Rotunda of The Natural History Museum is filled with elegantly dressed New Yorkers, chatting as they wait to enter the opening night of the exhibition. The invitees are special patrons, and they look the part with their designer outfits and expensive haircuts.

Nadir walks ahead of me to the front of the crowd. Our footsteps echo up to the high ceiling, where banners hang down, advertising coming attractions. When we reach the velvet rope, he flashes some sort of trustee's card, and the guard ushers us inside.

Although Nadir's outfit is undetectable in his natural habitat (the dorm), out in the wild he looks like an escapee from a teenage crossbreeding program, with elements of hip-hop, beatnik, and swing kid, with a dash of punk rock.

I, on the other hand, have tried to dress like an adult, in fitted slacks, a silk blouse, Chelsea boots, and some understated silver jewelry. At least I blend in with the crowd.

"This way." Nadir motions me along. "Wait until you meet Dr. Sullieman. He's beastly."

"He's what?"

"You know—gangsta."

"Can't wait."

Once again, Nadir's pants are so low I can't work out the physics of how they stay up. Finally, I break down and ask.

"How do your pants stay up, Nadir?"

He looks at me like I'm a fool. "They're sewn to my boxers."

"Then how do your boxers stay up?"

"How does your underwear stay up, Jenna?"

I shoot him back the same look, messing with him. "What underwear?"

He grins.

The sound of muffled voices, clinking glasses, and an exotic-sounding flute float down the wide hallway. We must be getting close. Just around the corner, people are gathering near an exhibit hall. A giant banner hangs above the doorway. The legend reads: *Bedouin Textiles: Weavers of the Desert.* As we walk inside, I'm struck by the raw beauty of the Bedouin Textile exhibit. Framed on the walls are examples of rugs, shawls, and wedding clothes in bright primary colors.

Next to the textiles are maps of the regions, cultural objects, and photographs of the various tribes. Weather-beaten faces stare out from the images, eyes blazing with life against leathery skin. Some of the pictures are old, from the turn of the century, others are sharp and modern.

The atmosphere is relaxed, like a cocktail party. People are milling around, leaning in to get a closer look and chatting with each other. It's all very civilized and pleasant.

A waiter offers us a tray of tiny sandwiches. I remember rule number five: *Eat when you can.* So I grab a few tidbits and wolf them down.

In the center of the room, a paunchy man in his mid sixties

with graying hair holds court. He's animated, dressed in a pale suit with a psychedelic tie. A black onyx ring set in gold rests on his pinkie. Tucked under his arm is a thick hardcover book, which he hands to interested parties now and then for inspection. He clearly loves being the center of attention. This must be Dr. Ben Adir Sullieman.

Nadir strides up, slouching, hands deep in his pockets "Dr. Sullieman, this is that grad student I spoke to you about? Jenna Stack."

Sullieman studies me carefully with eyes bulging out as if his thyroid gland is malfunctioning. His mustache, sideburns, and salt and pepper goatee are all lovingly manscaped. He holds out a fleshy hand as if presenting me with a prize. No humility here. None at all.

I shake hands and smile pleasantly. I'm here to extract information, not to pay homage. But I think I'll have to kowtow a little to succeed.

"You didn't tell me Jenna was so *lovely*," he oozes, rubbing my hand and giving me a look I can only describe as, *I've seen too many old James Bond movies and genuinely believe you'll be charmed by my sophisticated world-renowned expert schtick.*

Oh God. Really? I've had a hard enough week, what with the mugging, the FBI (if Cole really is FBI), and all the lizards and snakes. Now I have to navigate an interaction with this randy old goat?

The good news is I'm quite sure I can get his big ego working for me. I take a deep breath and try to ratchet the temperature of my pasted-on smile above freezing.

"Sir, what a pleasure. I've been told you're the leading expert on Bedouins in the entire world."

Sullieman licks his lips. He thinks Nadir has brought him a new toy to play with, a "lovely" Jenna doll.

"Why, you flatter me, dear."

I'm thinking to myself, yes, I do, because I want information, and you obviously like to be admired. But out loud I answer, "I doubt that."

"What do you wish to know?"

"I'm interested in the Zahar Tribe."

"Ah, the Zahar." He slides his arm through mine and caresses my hand again. I get a whiff of pungent cologne. "An ancient tribe, made up of seven primary family lines, possibly migrating to Saudi Arabia from Babylon, the area now known as Iraq."

Sullieman walks me over to an illustrated timeline spanning one large wall, plastered with photos. "These are the Bedouin tribes. We begin here, in the late eighteenth century. As you can see, tribal costumes have not changed much. They are dressed in their native—"

"Doctor, remember the family feud we discussed?" Nadir interrupts Sullieman before he gets too far onto the topic of clothing.

"The feud between the Zahar and the Ab El Maliks?" Sullieman replies, raising an eyebrow.

"Yes." I quickly reclaim my arm while he's distracted. "A name kept popping up in Nadir's research. Hussein Khalid?"

"AKA: Killer of the Firstborn Son," Nadir adds.

"Ah yes, Hussein Khalid. Well, now you've come to the heart of the feud, bright boy. I see why Wolfson touts you."

That's it. From this moment on I am going to assume every person I meet knows Wolfson.

Nadir grins. Clearly a sucker for a compliment, he is completely under this guy's spell.

"I'm afraid the story of Hussein Khalid is a tragedy. As headman of the Zahar, he was charged by Sheik Faisal Ab El Malik to guard his firstborn son, Bishr. During a particularly hazardous journey, Bishr was assassinated—on his watch."

"Killer of the Firstborn Son," Nadir whispers and turns to me. "There were originally seven brothers. Uncle Bishr was the eldest, not Mohammad. But Bishr was killed by rebel forces in the desert." He looks at Sullieman as if he has just produced a rabbit out of midair. "No one ever talks about it."

"Then what your family may not have told you is the day after Bishr was assassinated, Hussein Khalid was beheaded in the public square, then crucified."

Beheaded and crucified? That sounds a little like overkill, literally. I try to smooth out the crazy look on my face. I am calm. I am sophisticated. I can adult swim with the best of them. Bring it on, Professor Gross-Out.

"That is what started the blood feud," Sullieman says with a sigh. "There have been incidents between the two families ever since. The only thing that will satisfy a blood feud is death. Both families have lost a significant member."

"But wasn't Hussein protecting Bishr?" I ask.

"If you royally fuck up—like someone important gets killed on your watch—The Kingdom goes all medieval on your ass," Nadir explains, shaking his head.

Dr. Sullieman adds, "And there were rumors of treachery, although years later it was confirmed Hussein Khalid was not involved."

"Why would they behead him? And if he's already dead, nail him to a post?" I can't help asking, even as I feel the delicious tiny sandwiches I ate churn dangerously in my stomach.

Sullieman smiles at me as if I am a particularly stupid child. "My dear, not every country tries to rehabilitate criminals. Saudi Arabia still beheads and stones people on occasion. For example, in two thousand nineteen, there was a mass execution of thirty-seven Shia men after extracting their confessions of terrorism by torture. Amnesty International was less than pleased. In fact, when it comes to executions, the United States regularly hits the top twenty worldwide." Sullieman smiles as if his precious stories and depressing facts are polished rubies.

Is this his idea of seduction? Lecturing me about international execution law? He takes my arm again. I try not to cringe. We continue walking along the timeline.

"Here we have the tribes of Jordan: the Hajaya, the Rawalla, the Abbad. The tribes of Egypt and the Sudan—"

"What are these?" I point to some drawings: a pair of birds, a cross, and a scimitar.

"The Bedouins often sign textiles and documents with a symbol or crest. For example, this is the Zahar crest." He points to another symbol—two crossed swords over an eye.

I take my phone out and snap a picture.

"Ah, here we are." Sullieman steers me toward an old photograph. "The man you asked about, Hussein Khalid."

I slip away from the touchy academic to examine the sepia-toned image. Standing in front of a nomadic tent is a handsome man, dressed in flowing white robes. A pair of daggers is tucked into his belt. He has fierce eyes and a proud stance. Behind him is a younger man, sharp featured, with skin the color of iron.

"Who's this guy?" I point to the young man.

"His second in command, Ali Kabir. After Khalid's death, he became headman. He remains leader of what's left of the Zahar tribe to this day."

"*Ali Kabir*?" I try not to let my jaw drop. Nadir looks stunned too. So this is the man meant to sign for the briefcase with the hidden money? The same guy Adar Abassi laughed off, saying the sheik was like the CEO of Exxon who didn't know all his employees—including the new headman of the Zahar tribe? *That* Ali Kabir? What is going on with this crazy family?

I snap another picture and follow Sullieman as he walks us to the end of the timeline. He points at a color photo.

"This is the Zahar tribe today. Such a proud tribe. Such a pity."

Ali Kabir again, older, his face heavily lined but his eyes still sharp. The tribe members behind him are weather-beaten and shop-worn, bent under the weight of drudgery. They are posed in front of rusting tin shacks with scrawny goats wandering at their feet.

"What happened to them?"

"The Bedouins are transitioning to modern life, from small rural environments with tents, to cinderblock houses with central plumbing, television, cars, and pickup trucks. They've been marginalized, cut off without resources. But the Zahar have it far worse. They live in a village, unrecognized by their government, on the outskirts of a vast garbage dump."

Well, that's awful. And I thought *I* had accommodation problems.

"Where do things stand today?" Nadir says. "Does the blood feud still exist?"

"It's possible," Dr. Sullieman says. "I'd like to think those days are in the past, but blood feuds die hard."

"Is there any way to find out?" I ask directly.

"I suppose you'll know if someone dies," he responds dramatically, licking his blubbery lips.

I tug on Nadir's sleeve. Time to go.

"Thank you for your time." Nadir nods politely. "This has been very helpful."

"No trouble. Are you sure you won't stay for a drink, lovely Jenna?" The hopeful look in Sullieman's eyes is disturbing in so many ways. He strikes me as a fantastic grouper, waiting at the bottom of a small pond for a fish to come close enough so he can swallow it, scales and all.

"Er, no thanks. I have to wash my hair."

The traffic in the museum is thinning out. The line in the rotunda has disappeared, and the patrons are slowly drifting away into the night.

"Well, that was worth it, Nadir."

"I told you he knows his stuff."

Nadir and I meander toward the exit when something, or rather someone, catches my eye. The minute I register his presence, he slips out of sight, but not before I recognize the shadowy face from beneath the baseball cap the night of the mugging—Sasha Kurgan. If that thug was willing to shoot Adar Abassi, what else is he capable of? I need to get Nadir out of here, fast.

"Nadir, you need to leave."

He looks at me like I'm nuts. "What's wrong?"

"I'll explain later. Keep digging. Try to find out more about the blood feud and the money. Call you later?"

"Okay. Cool." He shrugs. "But text me, J. I'm not much for the phone."

I watch Nadir's figure grow smaller as he heads to the door. I'm glad he'll be safe, but I have no idea how I'm going to get myself out of here alive.

Chapter 22
Bioluminescence

Strange how things can change in an instant. Dr. Sullieman's unwanted advances seem a lot less annoying now that Sasha Kurgan has arrived. I take a few steps toward the safety of the rotunda, but before I can reach the milling people, Kurgan steps out from the shadows.

He's bigger than I remember, heavy and well-muscled, wearing what looks like a flak jacket. There's something in his hand. A blade catches the light. He smiles at me without humor, just a cold acknowledgment of my existence. And a promise that my future may be cut short.

The reception is over. Attendees are flooding in my direction, chatting and laughing, headed for the bottleneck at the main door. I fall in line with them. Kurgan follows, slipping into the crowd. I get the feeling, crowd or no crowd, he'll do something nasty.

As we round the corner, there's a roped-off exhibit with a sign that reads: *Bioluminescence: Strange Animals of the World.*

I slip beneath the velvet rope.

The exhibit hall is dark except for a series of fish tanks

whose occupants flicker with eerie blue light. Hugging the wall, I inch deeper into the shadows. Imagining Kurgan as an animal who can sense my fear, I hold my breath while I wait for him to pass.

Sure enough, he comes to the exact spot where I split off and stops. I will him to move along, follow the crowd, but he just keeps examining the entrance as if he's mapping the dark hallway. He bows his head for a moment, listening. Then his brow narrows and a murderous look appears on his face.

Kurgan slips under the rope too.

I retreat into the shadows, past the bubbling tanks. My heart pounds as he creeps toward me, heavy heels scuffing the marble floors. I back away, deeper into the darkness.

Up ahead is a winding ramp. I reach out until I feel the railing. The dark room hides my movements as I make my way down the incline. My eyes are adjusting to the darkness. At the end of the ramp is an open space. On the other side are exhibits and doors leading to galleries with plenty of places to hide, but the only way through is out in the open.

I hesitate, afraid to cross, even in the darkness. But Kurgan is creeping closer. I have no choice. As I step out onto the open space, the floor lights up.

I look down in horror.

The entire floor responds to my weight with ghostly puddles under my feet. You've got to be kidding me! I sprint across the open space, each footstep radiating a glowing trail.

Behind me, I hear the thud of Kurgan's boots.

I duck between display cases and into the next exhibit—a room full of summer fireflies. They float in the air behind glass displays, trailing languid arcs of light at odds with the grim situation. The air is so full of light, I'm completely exposed. I run across the floor to the next gallery, keeping low. A shadow steps into the doorway.

It's Kurgan, a black hole in a sea of swarming radiance, blocking the pattern of the fireflies.

I slip into the next gallery, lean against the wall, and catch my breath.

"Where are you, little girl? Can you hear me? I saw your footsteps. I offer payment for your silence."

Sure you do. I believe that as much as I'll believe Dave next time he claims to have an easy assignment for me.

This gallery is shaped like a vast cave. Luminous, silken lines dotted with light hang down from the ceiling. I spot a sign that reads: *Glowworms.* I move across the cavernous room, then crouch down and wait. I close my eyes, hoping to sense Kurgan's movement through the dark.

"Why do you run?" he calls out. Then a bizarre sound comes out of his throat, like a low growl. The hair on my arms stands up. I back up, passing into the next gallery.

A sparkling, bioluminescent sea opens on either side of the pathway. A plaque reads *Mosquito Bay: Puerto Rico.* Dave once had a boyfriend who kept promising to take him to see the glowing blue water.

The low growl comes again. I duck behind a tall case, afraid the light will expose me. This exhibit would be so awesome if I weren't being chased by a Russian hitman. And who knows if I'll live to come back and enjoy it? Jerk!

Everything's quiet, so I weave through a series of glass displays, crouching down until I reach the end of the exhibit and burst through a door into a well-lit hallway. Oh no! I'm completely lost and totally exposed. I run quickly and quietly across the floor, then press myself into a deep doorway, allowing the shadow to swallow me.

I steady my breath. Did I lose him?

As if on cue, Kurgan bursts through the door and looks in both directions. Please, please, please God. Let this knife wielding, growling lunatic go away. I promise to be good and mind my own business. Kurgan steps away. I hear his footsteps retreating. Then they stop. Oops. Did I really promise to mind my own business?

I peek around the door jam. Kurgan's standing in the wide hallway, deciding which way to go. There's a fifty/fifty chance he'll head in my direction. I can't stay here.

Going left is out of the question. I'll bump straight into Kurgan. Turning right means exposure in the bright hallway. One door over is an exhibit marked: *Animal Totems.*

As soon as Kurgan looks away, I dart through the open doorway.

Immediately, I'm engulfed by a forest of totem poles. Brightly colored bird and animal faces stare down with wide eyes, their carved tops disappearing into blackness. It's terrifying and beautiful at the same time. I weave around the poles, trying to find a place to hide. All I can do is try to find the biggest totem pole and wait.

"Where are you, little bird?" comes the growling voice. Sasha Kurgan begins circling. It's hard to tell where he is. The high ceiling distorts the acoustics. I almost bump into a snarling, sharp-toothed dragon face and begin to panic. My heart beats faster, breath punching in and out of my chest. The hitman's footsteps grow louder.

I run to another totem pole. There's got to be a way out. Think! Do I have any potential weapons? Why haven't I bought mace or a stun gun by now? Everything in my life seems to be like this— finding out the hard way. But in this case the hard way will mean a knife in the gut. I've got to think of something.

An arm grabs me. I try to scream, but a hand clamps over my mouth. A calm voice hisses in my ear, "Shhhhhhh." Then he pulls me deeper into the shadows.

I find myself looking into the steady green eyes of Cole Braedon. I don't know if he's here to help me or kill me, but his arm is viselike as he holds me against him. I'm not going anywhere. Slowly my breath falls in sync with his deep, calm rhythm. The heat from his body radiates against me. He smells spicy and delicious, like food you want to eat but are afraid won't agree with you.

Kurgan's footsteps slow down. I can tell by their sound, he's unsure. He taps a little bit this way, a little bit that, doubles back, uncertain. Maybe he heard something? Then he stops completely. There's nothing between us and him but twenty feet of shadow. I stop breathing. Time slows down. The heaviness is oppressive. Cole's heat is unbearable and weirdly thrilling.

Finally, Kurgan takes a step, then another, then a third. Is he? Yes. He's moving away from us. We remain there, rigid, until Kurgan's footsteps die away. Slowly, Cole takes his hand off my mouth, touching his lips to indicate silence. His hand traces the curve of my back in that subtle way where it could be an accident or on purpose. I begin to move away, but he pulls me against him. My hand rests lightly on his heart.

"Not yet," he warns softly.

His lips are inches from my mouth. I don't want to admit it, but everything about him is intoxicating. What is wrong with me? How on earth can I be attracted to this man, who is impersonating a dead Canadian and may or may not be an FBI agent?

The cell phone in Cole's pocket vibrates. He slips it out and turns the screen toward me so I can see Sasha is calling. He ignores it.

"Are you okay?" he asks.

"Fine." My voice is breathless. Please let him assume it's entirely because I'm scared and not partly because he's standing so close to me. A guy like this would use that information against me in the worst possible way.

"Come on." Cole pulls me out of the shadows. "This way."

We exit the totem pole exhibition, then backtrack through gallery after gallery of ancient artifacts until we come to a side door and slip out into the night. He's been here before.

Chapter 23
Cage the Canary

We're safely inside Cole's surveillance van. The interior is dark and quiet, with only the low whir of electronic equipment vibrating the air. Cole sits across from me, back pressed against the metal interior, eyes bright and intense. I can tell he's still wired. I'm winded, my nerves frazzled, but my mind is racing. I feel exhilarated.

"What is wrong with that guy? Why was he growling at me?" I brush a damp strand of hair away from my mouth.

Cole laughs and looks at me with appreciation. "Sasha kills people for money. He's a sadist and an animal. He can sense your fear, like a cat toying with his kill. He growls because he knows it's frightening."

"So if he's the cat, that makes me the mouse? Great," I joke and smooth out my blouse, then check that I still have my phone, and generally try to recover my dignity.

Cole's expression grows thoughtful.

"I don't think so, Jenna. I haven't decided what you are yet. But you're definitely not a mouse. What were you doing there, anyway?"

"Seeing an exhibit," I lie. "You?"

"We were sent to kill you. Again."

Well, that's awkward.

"Sorry I can't be more help with my own murder."

To my surprise, Cole laughs, which gets me laughing. There's a new current passing between us. More of a camaraderie. Like I passed some test. Every time our eyes meet, there's electricity. It's distracting. But it also makes me feel strong.

"How did you know I'd be here?"

"I didn't. Sasha knew."

Huh? Was I followed, or did someone tell him?

"Really, Jenna. Why were you there?"

"Following a lead. I went to see Professor Sullieman."

"What did you find out?"

"There's a blood feud between the Ab El Maliks and the Zahar tribe. Ali Kabir inherited the tribe from Hussein Khalid when Mohammad's father chopped Khalid's head off and nailed him to a board."

"Ouch. Doesn't explain why Abassi was dropping money to Kabir."

"No, but I don't think Abassi knew about the hidden money in the briefcase. He thought it was business as usual."

"Why didn't you upload Evan's hard drive?"

"I got interrupted."

Annoyance clouds his eyes. He doesn't believe me.

"Look Jenna, I've been doing this a long time. Evan is a link in the chain of that money. I know you want to protect your friend, or boyfriend, or whatever..."

"He's not my boyfriend."

"Evan could have information he doesn't know he has. He could be a psychopath for all you know."

Really, Evan a psychopath? I doubt that. And looks who's talking.

"If Evan Blake is a psychopath, what does that make you?"

His eyes burn, and I can't help but enjoy the reaction. I've hit a nerve. He looks angry. And really hot. Why do I enjoy challenging him?

"What do you mean by that?" he asks, his voice bordering on threatening.

"I mean, who is Cole Braedon? Besides some Canadian who died a decade ago?"

His jaw clenches. His eyes grow distant, unfocused.

The equipment in the van starts making a series of clicking noises. Without a word Cole, or whatever his name is, slips into the command chair and begins adjusting dials. A phone rings. A voicemail with no outgoing message picks up, followed by a beep and Sasha Kurgan's unmistakable voice.

"The yellow bird escaped. I will track and put in cage." The phone clicks and dies.

"Yellow bird?" I ask. "Does he mean canary? As in canaries sing?"

Cole turns back to me and shrugs. "Probably."

"I suppose 'put in cage' means kill?"

"I'm afraid so. In a few minutes, he'll get a call back with new orders."

"Who gives him the orders?"

"We don't know. Whoever it is uses a caller ID spoof card, puts up a different ID every time. And the signal is untraceable."

That seems like a dead end, so I bring the conversation back to his identity.

"Are you going to answer my question? Who are you, really?"

There's a trace of sadness in his eyes. "I've been Cole Braedon for so long now, I'm as much him as anyone else," he answers cryptically.

"Are you even FBI?"

He scowls at me this time as if my question is insulting. Considering he's the first FBI agent I've met, and he might be a faker, it doesn't seem terribly rude to ask.

"Has anyone ever told you curiosity can be detrimental to your health?"

"Yeah, I've heard that once or twice."

"How's Tyler? Has he heard back yet about the evidence? The new DNA test?"

"How do you know about that?"

Cole smirks and looks at me as if I'm naïve.

"All right, yes. He got a letter. They said the evidence was destroyed in a flood."

"And you believe that?"

Until this moment I hadn't considered the possibility the letter was anything other than genuine. Cole just stares at me, a curious look on his face.

"What do you mean? Like it's a fake or they're lying?"

"I'm torn. I sort of love the way you ask these questions, the purity of you." He leans forward and puts a thumb and finger under my chin, as if he's going to kiss me. My breath catches in my throat. Then he whispers, "Jenna, you have terrific instincts. But they betray you because you simply don't understand the nature of human beings."

"I have a degree in psychology—"

"You memorized a bunch of patterns with funny names. Out here, things are different. People are not so easily quantifiable."

The cold distance settles over his eyes again and he leans back. "Listen, Jenna. There are bad people in the world, people with terrible motivations. To those people, a kid like Tyler is nothing more than collateral damage. I told you I can help him, and I will. But you have to keep up your end of the bargain."

Oh no. We're back to this.

"Forget Evan's computer," he adds.

Oh thank goodness!

"You're going to the ball on Saturday, right?"

I nod. How does he know these things?

"While you're there, you can access the sheik's computer, which is even better. No URL this time. The main computer in his office isn't connected to the Internet."

Cole reaches into a dark recess of the van and pulls out a folded piece of paper. "Here's a floor plan of the house." He points to a room on the second floor. "This is Mohammad's office. There are two staircases. The grand staircase is right off the ballroom. You're going to need to get to this one." He points to a section of the house off the kitchen. Then he holds up what looks like a thumb drive but fatter. "And this will do the rest. When the light blinks, it's done. Then get out."

I look at him incredulously. Is he actually trying to get me killed at this point? Has he not seen the security at that house?

"Are you insane?" I stare at the floor plan.

"Jenna, this is our deal. If you do this for me and you don't tell anyone about it—"

"Yeah, right. Like I'd tell anyone."

"I promise you," he continues, "I will walk through fire to find a way to help Tyler."

He sounds sincere, passionate even. He also sounds like a total sociopath. And yes, I know that word is out of favor, but I like it, and I rarely get to make the diagnosis. Cole is everything my degree in psychology prepared me to be wary of. He is narcissistic, charming, sexual, confident, deadly, controlling, and obviously challenged in the empathy department. What primal part of me is responding to him? I shudder to think.

He holds up the drive, or whatever it is, and smiles. He knows he's got me. He knows I need his help. I take the device from his hand.

"Fine—but don't you dare back out on me."

The channel crackles to life again. There's a ring and a click as the phone picks up. A gravelly, unrecognizable voice says, "I don't care what you have to do. Lock up the canary. Permanently."

Damn voice-masking apps! Nowadays any suburban teenager can get technology more sophisticated than some governments. One thing is clear—somebody wants me dead.

Chapter 24
Crime Mapping

The idea of going to class today seems ridiculous. I mean, really? I've got a Russian gang after me, a sheik's computer to infiltrate, and I'm the reluctant asset of a *maybe* FBI agent. I'm also exhausted and paranoid. Last night I went through every inch of Andrea Billingsworth's apartment looking for bugs. How else could Cole know so much? We covered surveillance devices first semester, so I knew what to look for, mostly. I found nothing. Then I had to put the rooms back together and soothe the poor cats. I barely got any sleep.

I considered skipping Wolfson's lecture. But I want to ask him what he knows about Cole and if he's learned anything more from Sergei.

The topic today is crime mapping. Wolfson projects an elaborate map of New York City, covered with various emblems denoting the number and type of crimes. He's lecturing about contributing factors, areas of prostitution, drugs, gang territories. It can be hard to follow Wolfson on a good day. Today I'm just lost. All I can think about is my conversation with Cole last night. How did he know about the latest developments in Ty's case? About my invitation to the ball? And who the hell is he, really?

I make eye contact with Wolfson during the lecture. I think I've communicated my need to talk to him. Finally, he excuses the class. "I expect you to finish the reading assignment before our next meeting. And Miss Stack, my office please."

I've never been to Wolfson's office. I follow him down the hall to a room that looks pretty much how I imagined; dark, musty, and full of junk. Graphic crime scene photos are casually strewn over an old metal desk. A collection of acrylic paperweights with bugs encased in them gathers dust on a shelf. Bookshelves sag with the weight of volumes on a dizzying array of subjects. A tweed couch that couldn't possibly be school issue, and several chairs that clearly are, fill the room. A small flat screen TV sits on an end table, turned on and tuned in to New York 1 News. The anchorman is recounting the details of a multi-fatality house fire.

"Do come in and sit down." Wolfson gestures to a seat and closes the door behind me. He rubs his hands together, positively oozing drama and intrigue. "Tell me everything!"

Oh jeez. How much time have you got? It's been less than forty-eight hours, and I've been kidnapped by a cop, coerced by a possible FBI agent, charmed by a Saudi sheik, hit on by a creepy historian, and chased by a hitman—again.

I don't even know where to begin!

I give him a brief rundown, confirming that Cole Braedon is indeed Dimitri Solonik, but leaving out the part about being asked to break into every computer in town.

Wolfson laughs and nods with appreciation at my story. Finally I ask the question I've been saving up.

"What do you know about Cole Braedon, Professor?"

"Not much." Wolfson leans back in his chair and steeples his hands. "I've only met him a few times—professionally. But I do think he can be trusted. I was quite surprised when he called about you. And then to learn he is our mysterious Dimitri Solonik? He alters his appearance quite deftly."

I lean in. "He's not *just* Dimitri Solonik—according to Nadir, the name Cole Braedon belongs to a dead Canadian."

"Another fake identity?" For a moment, Wolfson looks both impressed and puzzled. Then he shrugs. "Don't judge our mysterious Mr. Braedon too harshly. You may have to change your identity before life is through with you. Measure the man by his actions, not his name."

"His actions? Well, Cole Braedon has a way of... getting around."

"But does he have a way of getting things done?" Wolfson looks at me with narrowed eyes. "I would say yes."

"What if he asks me to do something... dangerous?"

"Danger is relative."

That's a good point.

"You seem to have an unusually high threshold, dear."

Goody for me.

"Remember rule number three. The truth is in the details. No clue is too small. Trust your instincts. These go hand in hand. Listen to your gut."

What if all my gut wants to do is throw up?

Wolfson leans back, studying my face. "What are your instincts telling you?"

"I don't trust Cole Braedon." Yes, I lust him, but that is beyond my control.

"That's a start." Wolfson steeples his hands again and zones in on me with his fierce, laser eyes. "You will have to collaborate in your career, Jenna. Especially when you are in danger. I think Braedon wants the same thing you do—to get to the bottom of this puzzle."

"I guess so," I admit reluctantly. "So far, he's had my back."

Wolfson drums his fingers, waiting for something, so I keep going.

"But I don't know who has his back."

"Excellent point." Wolfson's phone buzzes. He glances down but ignores it. "What about the briefcase mystery? Any thoughts? Or has Mr. Braedon disrupted your mind so completely you can't focus?"

Grrrr. Wolfson just loves to push buttons. One of these days I'm going to find his ripcord and pull.

"Something strange is definitely going on with Bokra International. But I really don't think Evan is involved."

"Then who?"

"Whoever is sending money to Ali Kabir."

Now that I think about it, getting into the sheik's computer might uncover some new information, or new players.

"Who do you suspect?"

"Abassi was acting strange at the hospital, like he knew something. Not really suspicious, but strange."

"Perhaps you should go back and speak with him. Alone this time. Be prepared with your questions. Push him. See if anything sets off your nerves."

Yes! Go back, alone, and speak with Adar. That idea agrees with my gut.

"And Jenna?" Wolfson speaks in a serious tone. "Sasha Kurgan is still at large and may be growing suspicious of Mr. Braedon. Since whoever is behind this case remains invisible, you may want to revisit rule number two."

"Trust no one," I whisper as I slip out of the room.

Chapter 25
A White Rose

On the way to visit Adar Abassi at Mount Sinai, I have Tyler on my mind. His situation seems so hopeless. I'm beginning to care less about who Cole is exactly, as long as he can help my brother.

The reception area of Eleven West Wing is cool and quiet. A pretty, red-headed attendant greets me. She's wearing a beige vest and striped tie against a crisp, starched shirt, beige skirt, and white nurses' shoes. Is she a concierge or a healthcare worker? I lean on the marble countertop adorned with fresh flowers and write my name on a sign-in sheet.

"Yes, Miss Stack. You're approved to visit our Mr. Abassi. Go right in."

Our Mr. Abassi? They must love him. He pays full price, and he's charming.

I have so many questions. Abassi may remember more details about Ali Kabir or know something about the Zahar tribe. Or he might just be able to give me names of people to talk to. I knock on Abassi's door. No response. I push the door open.

"Mr. Abassi?" I step inside and shut the door. The guards are missing. Have they been called off? I walk through the sitting room.

Adar Abassi is in bed, lying on his side. His eyelids flutter and he looks at me and squints, as if his vision is blurry.

"Where are your guards?" I indicate the empty room.

"I dismissed them." His color is sallow. He doesn't look good. Has there been some sort of complication?

"Are you all right? How are you feeling?"

He looks at me with tired eyes and nods.

"I'm so glad you've come, Miss Stack," he says gently and shudders. "I was hoping you would come."

"Please, call me Jenna."

He seems to be in a cold sweat. Cold? Pain? Doped up on meds? I'm not sure, but something feels really wrong. "Listen, I wanted to ask you some questions, but they can wait—"

"No. Ask. I insist." He beckons me closer. "You must ask me *now*."

I step by the side of his bed, nervously. "Have you heard of a man named Hussein Khalid?"

His eyes roll up for a moment, then settle into a basilisk stare. "Of course."

"Then you know Ali Kabir was his lieutenant, and he leads the Zahar tribe?"

"And that I have been delivering money to a sworn enemy of the Ab El Maliks? Yes."

Okay. Now we're getting somewhere.

"Why is that?"

He coughs. A tremor moves through his limbs.

"You are picking the scab of a dangerous secret, Jenna. One you'd be safest not to reveal." His body shakes again. He's drenched in sweat.

"Are you sure you're all right?"

"We don't have much time." He looks at me, his eyes filling with tears. "Come closer."

He takes my hand. His arm is swollen and purple.

"We need to get you help!" I look around for the call button, but he squeezes my hand hard.

"Please! You must tell Evan—his life depends on this—to run. Now. Leave this place, this city. You too. I cannot enter paradise carrying your deaths in my heart."

A trickle of blood runs from his nose. He lets go of my hand, takes a labored breath, then coughs violently. Blood sprays across the sheets and foams from his mouth.

I find the call button tangled in a rat's nest of cords hanging off the bed. I press it again and again then run to the door and fling it open.

"HELP! HELP!"

A nurse runs past me into the room. Abassi is grimacing, convulsions running through his body, dark blood soaking the sheets, spreading around his head, and coating his teeth. The heart monitor races faster, then slows, as if his heart is struggling to find its rhythm. The nurse picks up the phone and shouts into the receiver.

Within seconds the speakers blare out, "Code Blue," followed by the room number. Everything speeds up.

A crash team bursts through the door. They cut off Abassi's clothing. The doctor starts chest compressions and yells, "Get her out of here!"

An orderly pushes me into the hallway. I lean against the wall, helplessly watching through the open door.

Different voices shout ominous words: *Hemorrhaging! Asystole! IV! Suction! Paddles!*

A doctor yells, "Clear!" They jolt Abassi over and over.

Then his body lies still, and the silence lengthens.

Finally, the doctor says, "I'm calling it. TOD one-ten p.m."

I slide down the wall, sinking and burying my head in my hands. What just happened? One second Adar Abassi was talking. The next he was dying—horribly. And it didn't look like a natural death to me.

I must have been there for a while, because when I look up, a familiar figure is approaching. I recognize the rigid, determined gait.

Detective John Denning is dressed in combat green khakis, a black T-shirt, and black windbreaker to cover his gun. His badge dangles from a chain around his neck. When he sees me, his face changes. Not for the better.

"I should've known," he says. "You're a homing pigeon for trouble."

"I wouldn't go in there if I were you."

Denning peeks through the open door at Abassi in his hospital bed. There is something disturbingly incongruous about the man's violent end juxtaposed with the luxurious room. The doctor walks out, shaking his head, followed by nurses and the code team. Denning turns to me. "Wait here. Do not move." Then he takes the doctor aside to question him. They keep glancing over at me.

I try to catch my breath. Tears stream down my cheeks. I can't believe this happened. Why did it happen? I need to see him again. I step back into the room. Adar Abassi is covered in a bloody sheet. I pluck a white rose from a flower arrangement and place it on his body.

A nurse walks in to remove the crash cart. "I'm so sorry."

"Me too."

"He was a gentleman," she adds.

The late afternoon light streams through the window, emphasizing the eerie stillness.

I call Evan. He answers on the first ring.

"Evan, listen, I have some difficult news."

He's silent at first.

"What kind of news?" he says warily.

"Adar Abassi is dead."

There is a muffled choking sound.

"B-but how can that be? I just saw him this morning."

There's no good way to say the next words out of my mouth, so I just blurt it out.

"Listen Evan, I think someone killed him."

There is a deep wall of silence as he mulls over my words.

"Are you certain?"

"He tried to warn me to run—leave the city. He knew something, but he died before he could tell me. I wasn't that scared before. Now I am. You need to leave town."

More silence, followed by a weak voice. "I can't, Jenna, not until after the fête."

The Faux Fur and Furry Friends Fête? Seriously?

"Are you kidding, Evan? I am standing in a room with a dead man, and you want to go to a pet party?"

"Fatima can't cancel it now. I have to go, Jenna. It's expected."

"But someone is running around killing people—"

"We don't know that yet. Let's wait and see what the police have to say. Besides, I'm not going to let down Mohammad."

"What if Mohammad is behind this?"

"I don't believe that. And I don't think you do either."

A restless shadow falls across the door. Denning is back. He looks at me, and there's a warning in his eyes.

"Listen, I have to go. I'm sorry about your friend."

Evan's voice softens. "Me, too."

Chapter 26
Matzo Ball Soup

Denning is brooding and angry as we walk down the hall. But as soon as he sees the reception desk, he changes his personality instantly: flashing badge, dazzling grin, flirtatious. He leans on the desk, emanating a sultry, masculine presence, and in a New York minute, the red-headed attendant hands Denning the sign-in sheet.

They chat as he looks down the list, but I can't hear what they're saying. I feel as if I'm in a fog, still reeling from what I've just witnessed.

The attendant makes Denning a copy of the sheet, hands him the paper, then flicks her hair away from her face flirtatiously. Denning gives her his full attention, locking onto her gaze until she blushes. Then he slides her a business card, walks away, and grabs my arm.

Denning steers me out of the hospital and across the street to a coffee shop. We slide into a booth and face each other. Johnny Cash plays over the speakers as the waitress takes our order.

"Coffee." He looks across the table, sizing me up. "You're still shaky. You need to calm down. Tea?" he suggests, a hint of concern in his steady blue eyes.

"Sure," I nod, still rattled and relieved someone is deciding things for me.

He turns to the waitress. "Herbal tea for her. And some matzo ball soup."

"Matzo ball soup?"

"It'll help hydrate you."

I nod. Soup does sound good, but Denning's priorities are confusing. And why is he being so nice to me?

"What are we doing here, Denning? Don't you need to secure the scene? Call forensics?"

"There has to be a crime first, Jenna."

"But you saw the way Abassi died—"

"Look, I'm sorry you had to witness that, but there is no crime —not yet."

"But all the blood. It was horrible."

"He was a sick man, Jenna. We'll have to wait for an autopsy to know cause of death for sure. But in the meanwhile, we can ask questions." He pushes the sign-in sheet across the table. "Have a look at this. In addition to you, Abassi was visited by J. Jones and D. Bennet."

"Who are they?"

"The receptionist remembers one of them. Male, late forties, medium build, six feet tall. The other one, not at all. She must have been on break. We're following up. Checking everyone who had access to the wing. Questioning staff."

Our order arrives. I take a minute to sip my tea. My hand is shaking and my mind isn't working. Images of Adar Abassi dying keep intruding.

Denning pulls off his jacket. "Put this on." He helps me push my hands through the sleeves. "You're in shock."

"I'll be fine…"

He shakes his head, then pushes the soup closer. I take a sip. The broth is salty and delicious, the warmth comforting.

"So, what were you doing there exactly?"

People sure have been asking me that a lot lately. "Long story," is all I offer.

"I've got time." He smiles, a softer, kinder smile than the one he used on the receptionist.

"What about you? I thought this was Cole Braedon's case?"

"Listen Jenna. I don't like being told to drop cases. And I wasn't happy delivering a civilian to climb into a van with an undercover agent with a death wish." His expression is earnest, sincere. "This is still my case, so why don't you just tell me what's going on?"

Denning leans in and holds my gaze with an intensity that makes me feel vulnerable, exposed. Maybe I am in shock. I'm paranoid, that's for sure. What if this is some kind of test to see if I'll reveal my exchange with Cole? Could they be working together? Still, Denning is a cop, and I have important information that could shed light on Abassi's death.

"That mugging wasn't a mugging."

"What was it then?"

"A hit."

"Do you even know what that means?"

"At this point, I have a pretty good idea."

"Who ordered this supposed hit?"

"The Russian mafia."

The concerned expression vanishes from Denning' face. Now he just looks exasperated.

"Why would the Red Mafia want to kill an accountant and a courier?"

"I'm not sure yet. But there's a blood feud going on."

"A blood feud?"

I nod solemnly. "I guess I didn't really believe it until now."

"And who is involved in this blood feud?"

"The Zahar Tribe and the Ab El Maliks."

Denning seems stunned. He looks me over like he's searching for clues, then starts a series of rapid-fire questions. I tell him as much as I can, leaving out the fact that I'm working as an informant for Cole to save my brother.

By the time I'm done, Denning has sunk into that state of low boil just before the lid flies off a pot. I can tell by the way he's grinding his teeth and flexing his arm muscles that he's about to blow.

"So you're telling me that jerk Braedon almost got you killed by the Russian mob? Did he send you to question Abassi? To get answer for him without exposing his identity?"

"Actually, talking to Abassi was my idea. And Wolfson's. Braedon doesn't even know I was there." Good call not telling him about the computer stuff.

"Finish your soup. I'm going to drive you home. And from now on, I want you to stay out of this. Do you understand me?"

I sip the tea and soup alternately while staring at him. That's a promise I can't make.

"Go to the bar. Walk dogs—not Evan Blake's. Do whatever it is you do. But steer clear of Blake and Braedon and the Ab El Maliks."

A vein in his forehead is bulging. As his intensity rises, my focus softens. I feel like I'm watching him through a haze.

"Do you understand me, Jenna?"

I nod yes. If I don't actually answer him out loud, am I technically lying?

"If something comes up, you call me immediately. If you can't get me, call Wolfson. I don't care what anyone says, I'm back on this case." He's like a caffeinated Boy Scout, and it's making me feel a little better. "And I won't let anything happen to you."

It's possible not all cops are bad. And it's possible I should have confided in him a lot sooner.

Denning drops a wad of bills on the table and storms toward the exit. I follow him out, not too proud to accept his offer of a ride.

My feline roommates hear me open the door and come running. There's nothing in the world like the unconditional love of an animal, or six. I feel a rush of gratitude that they're here and they need me. I lock the door and sit down in the entryway. Tigger jumps in my lap. Marmalade gets up on his hind legs and rubs his cheek against my face. Bram attacks my shoelace. They may just want food, but something about their outpouring of attention and affection sets me off.

Tears start flowing, then quickly turn into sobs—heaving, gut-wrenching, sobs. I let myself go. A trip to the bathroom mid-cry to get tissues leads me to the bed. I lie down and the whole gang follows. They seem to know I need the support.

A roll of TP later—all cried out and covered in fur—my mind finally begins to slow and all I can think about is Abassi's warning. What should I do? I could go upstate. Dave and Sharon would cover work for me. Wolfson, hopefully, would understand. Denning would be happy. But do I really want to just take off?

My deepest instincts tell me that's what a coward would do— slink off to safety, cover her own butt.

Then there's Tyler. Cole promised to help Tyler, but only if I access Mohammad's computer. How hard could that be, with everyone distracted at the party? I dig the floor plan Cole gave me out of my purse. The second floor is a circular maze off the grand staircase, with doors connecting room to room. Mohammad's office is clearly marked on one end.

The reality is the party is the nexus of this whole crazy situation. On the most basic level, blowing off the party is just plain rude. I'd be leaving an empty seat at the host's table. I may not be Miss Manners, but I do try to be polite.

Then again, is breaking into the host's computer polite? Definitely not. But that can't be helped. Tyler trumps everything else.

That leaves Evan. I'm not sure how I feel about him, exactly. Is he interested in me? Are we friends? Or does he just see me as the help? And would I even be attracted to him if we weren't thrown together in this bizarre situation? I don't know. But I do care what happens to him. And of all the people caught up in this situation, he is by far the least capable of taking care of himself. He's going to that party no matter what. If he's in danger like Abassi said, someone needs to keep an eye on him.

Angel appears in my peripheral vision and lets out a yowl that says, "Okay. You seem to have pulled it together. How about dumping some of that wet stinky slop we call food into my dish now!" I give her a rub and get up. Food all around.

Once the cats are taken care of, I realize I'm hungry too. I pop a frozen single serving of low-cal lasagna in the microwave and open a bottle of red wine. I'm about to save the cork, but who am I kidding? I toss it in the trash and commit to the bottle. While I wait for the microwave to ding, I text Dave, trying to keep it light.

Me: *Hey boss!*
Dave: *What have you been up to?*
Me: *Long story. Guess who's joining you at the social event of the season?*
Dave: *Who?*

Me: *Me! Scored an invite to the furry fête! I even get to stay for dinner!*

Dave: *Impossible! How?*

Me: *Looks like Honey's mom has taken a liking to me. Help me get ready?*

Dave: *Sure, Cinderella. I'll be your fairy godfather.*

Me: *Great! I'll tell Evan to swing the limo by your place. We'll all ride together.*

Dave: *You're turning out to be employee of the year!*

With that settled, all I have left to do is study the mansion floor plan, eat my dinner, get a good night's sleep and, of course, stay alive until tomorrow night.

Chapter 27
Mystery Box

I never went to prom in high school, the only other occasion when I would have primped for something special or fancy. So I take Dave's word that I need to get to his place two hours early. It's probably a good idea, since I have no idea what I'm going to wear.

When I arrive, there are two platters of hors d'oeuvres on the kitchen counter and an open bottle of champagne on ice. Dave is already dressed in a dashing tux with a splashy paisley bow tie, his jacket draped over a chair. I reach for a cracker and Dave slaps my hand.

"Not until you've showered. Now go."

I head for the bathroom with Dave calling out orders behind me. "Use the mineral scrub and the shampoo in the copper bottle."

I wash off the grime and craziness of yesterday, then wrap myself in a terry robe and head back to the living room. I dive into the snacks, downing a delicious deviled egg in one bite.

"Don't overeat. You don't want to spoil your appetite. But do graze. You don't want to show up hungry. And don't worry. It's all very bland. Nothing that could cause a breath issue or an upset stomach." Clearly, he's done this before.

He pours champagne into a flute and hands it to me. This is kind of fun. "Two drinks maximum before we leave. You want to arrive relaxed, not drunk."

I'm raising the glass to my lips when he shouts, "WAIT!" and grabs it out of my hand. "You didn't take any allergy pills today, did you? We don't want you falling asleep."

"No, totally drug-free."

"Okay. Proceed." He lets go of the flute.

The television is on for background noise, and a familiar face catches the corner of my eye.

"Is that Susie?" I point at the TV. A perky blonde holding a toy poodle is waiting to be interviewed by a spray-tanned former Miss New Jersey.

Dave rolls his eyes. "It's killing me that Susie's PetLove is sponsoring the fête this year." We both plop down on the couch with our champagne to heckle Dave's arch nemesis. "Look at that pink suit," Dave says. "Bad Chanel knock-off meets bubble-gum ice cream." He turns up the volume.

"What do you have planned for the Faux Fur and Furry Friends Fête this year?" Miss New Jersey says.

"Well, Amy," Susie beams, "I can't get into specifics. I'm sworn to secrecy. But I can tell you it's going to be *fur-abulous!* As the premiere pet service in all of New York City, we're thrilled to be a part of it."

"UGH! Fur-abulous. Really?" Dave tsks.

I giggle and sip my champagne.

"Well, you heard it here, folks. We expect nothing less than *fur-abulous* from hostess Fatima Ab El Malik. And with the help of Susie's PetLove, we can only imagine what surprises are in store for partygoers this year. Back to you, Marcus."

Marcus, a former child star with excessive dimples, wraps up the non-story with, "Thanks, Amy. Thanks, Susie. That poodle sure is cute. Of course, we'll have all of the red-carpet fashions and latest gossip from the party on the next Daily Dish."

"I can't stand that woman!" Dave laments.

"I know! I know! But just think. Next year it will be you being interviewed. This year you can spy and just have fun."

Dave downs his champagne, refills and downs another. "I'm allowing myself three!"

I'm not about to argue.

He shudders as if shaking off a bad feeling and thankfully switches gears. "So what's in the box?"

"What box?"

Dave points to a box on the couch that I assumed was for him. The package is large and white and tied with a gold ribbon. I walk over and see a card tucked in the ribbon, addressed to *Miss Jenna Stack, Tails of the City*, with Dave's address scrawled underneath.

No note. No signature.

"A messenger brought it by earlier."

I wasn't expecting anything. Is it a bomb? I'd feel terrible if Dave was collateral damage in the grand plan to cage this canary. Acting nonchalant, I give the delivery a cursory inspection. It's light. Bombs have some heft to them, don't they? It isn't sealed, just a large white gift box with a gold satin ribbon. I run a finger under the edges of the box. No wires. I lift it up to my ear. I don't hear anything. I give it a sniff.

"What are you doing?" Dave looks at me like I'm crazy.

"Checking for anything suspicious. You know, practice for school?"

"Seriously? Is this what I have to look forward to? A lifetime of you checking packages for who knows what?"

Sadly, he might be right, but I laugh it off as if I'm just being silly.

"Here, give it to me!"

Before I can protest, he rips the box from my hands, unties the ribbon and pulls off the lid. He tosses the box aside and pulls out the prettiest dress I've ever seen. It's seafoam green with short fluttery sleeves and little touches of lace and rhinestones. But the effect isn't tacky or frilly. It's absolutely lovely.

Dave checks the tag. "This is a Mason Dupree, Jenna. It's couture!" He looks at me in shocked surprise. I don't know who Mason Dupree is, but I know what couture means—expensive.

"Who sent it?" he demands, gesturing toward the box.

I check it inside and out. There's no note anywhere. Just the card with my name and Dave's address.

"I don't know. Maybe Evan?" Who else could it be?

"Jenna, this dress cost more than a Furry Fête dinner ticket."

"No!" I gasp. I wish he hadn't told me that—now on top of my paranoia of Russian hitmen, I'll be worried about ruining this dress.

"Well? Try it on!"

He passes me the glittery, filmy dress. The fabric is as light as a butterfly.

"I can't wear this!" I protest. "It's too extravagant! What if I ruin it?"

Dave crosses his arms and rolls his eyes. "What else are you going to wear? I've been dreading having to dig through your clothes and put something together all day."

He has a good point.

"At least see if it fits."

I duck into the next room. Slipping into the dress is like wrapping myself in a cloud. I step out and Dave zips me up. The fabric pulls together snugly. It fits perfectly.

Dave looks me up and down. I brace myself for a catty comment about my usual attire or how awkward I look. Instead, his eyes soften. "Oh Jenna. You look absolutely gorgeous."

And I must admit it feels great. I dig up a pair of silver shoes I wore in a wedding party once and Dave surprises me with an approving smile. I put on the heart necklace Cintia gave me. Dave does a little magic with my hair and makeup, and with five minutes to spare, we're ready to go.

When Evan doesn't show up on time, Dave tosses back another glass of champagne. He's a little giddy when the door finally buzzes, signaling it's showtime.

"Wait, wait! One more thing!"

Dave runs into his office and emerges with a jewel-encrusted clutch.

"This was in the gift bag at the GLAAD Awards."

He opens it under my nose and points to the Swarovski label.

"It's perfect for your outfit. Can I trust you to borrow it?"

I nod, dazzled by its sparkle.

While Dave collects his things, I carefully hide the spy-tech device Cole gave me and the mansion floor plan in the zippered lining of my borrowed clutch. Even though I've memorized the map, I feel better having it close at hand. On top I throw the usual —phone, compact, lip gloss.

Dave comes back, adjusting his fitted shirt. He looks me over and waves an imaginary fairy godfather wand before walking me to the full-length mirror. "Abracadabra! Don't you dare be home by midnight!"

I'm amazed by my reflection. This is, by far, the best I've ever looked. If I die tonight, leave me just as I am for the viewing.

Chapter 28
The Faux Fur & Furry Friends
Fête

Evan looks dashing standing next to the sheik's white limo in his formal tuxedo. Best of all, when he sees me, his jaw drops just the tiniest bit before he smiles and holds open the door.

"Ooh! Nothing like a handsome man in formal wear," Dave says. "Let's get a picture first!" He takes a photo of Evan and me standing in front of the limo. I'm embarrassed but kind of glad. I may never look this good again.

I climb inside the limo. The interior is lush, with soft white leather seats, subtle lighting, a fully stocked bar, and a drop-down video screen.

Settling myself on flouncy layers of fabric, I feel a bit like a puffed-up soufflé. The crystal clutch is firmly on my lap, and I trace the outline of the device I'm supposed to use to access Mohammad's computer. My stomach lurches from nerves—and maybe a few too many of Dave's deviled eggs. I wonder how spies like Valerie Plame managed to operate undercover, sometimes for years.

Evan slides in beside me, followed by Dave, and signals to the driver we're ready to go. The limo pulls into traffic.

"You look beautiful, Jenna." Evan brushes my hand lightly with his fingers.

"Thank you."

"What about me?" Dave jokes. "I exercised, exfoliated, and exceeded my champagne allotment."

He's buzzed, but Evan handles him beautifully. "You, too, are a vision, David. And please forgive my tardiness."

I fluff up my skirt. "And thank you for the dress."

He looks at me quizzically. "The dress?"

Okay. That answers that question. Evan didn't send it. I try to catch Dave's eye but he's busy checking his phone. "I mean for liking my dress. You know. It's always hard to know what to wear."

"You really don't know how beautiful you are, do you?"

I blush, not sure how to reply. It's a good thing Dave is here as a chaperone. Between Evan's compliments and hand touching, I'm getting ideas.

As the limo glides along the streets of New York, Dave and Evan chat about Max and this year's menswear collections. I nod as if I'm listening while trying to contain my alternating feelings of excitement and dread. As we round the last corner, you can tell there's a party going on. A small security force is stationed outside the mansion alongside a crew of parking valets.

The house is completely lit up. When we emerge from the limo, we are assaulted by paparazzi flashes. I have to admit, with my fur-abulous outfit, gracious imaginary boyfriend on one arm, and very real best friend on the other, I feel like the luckiest girl in the world.

But Wolfson is a firm believer in keeping a low profile and not attracting attention to oneself. No doubt I'm violating one of his rules just by walking through the front door. So while I'm giddy on the inside, I try to appear more like a jaded society partygoer than a girl who never went to prom.

We pass through security. The device in my purse doesn't trigger any alarms. A hostess checks us against a list, then sends us toward the front door. Fatima, in a regal purple gown and Mohammad in traditional robes, greet guests in the foyer. When we finally make our way to the front of the line, Mohammad looks pointedly at his heavy gold watch and shoots Evan a disapproving glance.

"I know. I'm sorry," he apologizes.

"We were just about to go in. Fatima needs to prepare to welcome the guests formally," Mohammad replies sternly. Evan nods and the sheik breaks into a smile, signaling we're not in too much trouble. They really do interact like family.

The sheik turns to me. "Jenna, you look stunning." I want to thank him for the dress, just in case he sent it, but the line moves so quickly I don't have time.

"Oh yes." Fatima looks me up and down approvingly. "Welcome. You are a vision, Jenna. So nice to see you again."

I don't even have a chance to compliment her. The elaborately carved oak doors open, and we follow a stream of people into the grand ballroom. As my eyes recover from the flashbulbs and adjust to the new environment, I notice that wife number two is missing.

"Where's Cintia?" I ask Evan.

"We Americans can be so judgmental of other cultures, and Fatima is the official hostess," he explains. "Better to have just one wife at the door. I'm sure she'll turn up later."

The ballroom is breathtaking. The first thing that strikes me is the sheer size. The room looks bigger tonight. I feel like I've walked into one of those Harry Potter illusions where a football-field sized room is made to fit inside a normal one, at least normal by rich New York society standards. Brightly patterned cloisonné vases as big as refrigerators hold lush arrangements of white orchids, gardenias, and lilies. Gold-framed mirrors emphasize the vastness of the space and reflect the well-heeled partygoers.

The cocktail reception is in full swing. Tuxedoed gentleman and their perfectly coifed dates pluck tiny hors d'oeuvres from passing golden trays while sipping from cut-crystal champagne flutes. A smattering of girls in flashy outfits—starlets, reality starlets, wannabe starlets—flutter around in search of attention. I notice a senator, a late-night talk show host, and a popular self-help guru. A cascade of peeping sounds makes me look up. Suspended overhead are a dozen delicate cages, holding a mix of brightly colored birds.

Many of the guests have pets with them. Dogs, cats, bunnies, even an iguana. Some animals are on leashes, others are being held by their owners. Trays with pet treats are also being passed around. Golden bowls of water are strategically placed under tables and in out-of-the-way spots. There is a little booth set up with six adorable puppies and a pamphlet with the heading, *Give a Homeless Pet a Chance—Adopt!*

Dozens of attendants in Susie's PetLove T-shirts are on hand to help with the animals. Then I see her. Ms. PetLove herself, dressed in an insanely gaudy gold lamé evening dress with faux leopard trim.

I catch Dave's eye. The publicity alone would have been worth doing this gig for free.

"I'm going to do some recon," Dave says, then off he skulks, fresh drink in hand, to spy on the competition.

Evan whispers, "I need to check in with Mohammad. Back in

five." He kisses my cheek, which I could really get used to, and disappears.

I hadn't expected to be on my own so quickly, but I'm relieved. Time to casually work my way toward that back staircase.

One third of the ballroom is blocked off by silk screens. I peek behind one of the barriers. Rows of banquet tables are set up with creamy-white tablecloths and floral centerpieces. The attractive blonde who consulted with Fatima and Cintia the day we had tea is supervising a gaggle of younger women, who bustle about, applying the finishing touches to the place settings for the formal dinner.

As I circle casually toward the back staircase, I accept a glass of champagne and a little canapé. Salty, smoky, and creamy all at once, it's delicious.

Above the ballroom, a series of arched balconies connects a labyrinth of rooms. A grand staircase leads to the second floor and the offices of Bokra International.

A murmur shudders through the crowd.

Fatima Ab El Malik descends the stairs, carrying Honey, the white Maltipoo. This must be the formal greeting the sheik mentioned.

Fatima's presence fills the room. Her natural charisma reminds me of Sophia Loren. Halfway down the steps, she stops and nods to the crowd. A hush falls over the guests.

"Welcome, everyone, to the fifth annual Faux Fur and Furry Friends Fête. Thank you for coming. I won't depress you with statistics." She smiles warmly, and a ripple of laughter echoes through the crowd. "Suffice it to say that as pet lovers, we need to end abuse and homelessness for our furry friends. And with your help, we *will*."

A few people lift their glasses in a sort of "power to the pets" salute as Fatima kisses Honey, who licks her cheek. The crowd oohs and aahs at the adorable Maltipoo as Fatima gestures toward an arched doorway on the far side of the ballroom.

"A silent auction is ongoing in the library, where you can also make a tax-deductible gift to the foundation. Dinner will be served promptly at nine. Enjoy yourselves!"

Fatima continues her descent, triggering a loud round of applause. A portion of the group drifts toward the library, while others surround her, eager for more time with the famous philanthropist. She steps onto the floor, shaking hands and smiling, at ease with her celebrity.

With so much going on, it's the perfect time to slip away. I toss back the rest of my champagne for liquid courage. Then I follow a woman in a red sequin gown clutching a miniature schnauzer. She heads toward a large, grass-filled patio off of the ballroom. The sign above the door reads "Pet Lounge."

Inside, there's a fenced-in dog run with toys, scratching posts, and pillows. Behind a fake hedge is a row of kennels, which I assume is a doggie "time out" area for misbehavers or pets that wander. Another handful of Susie's PetLove attendants are on hand. But they're too busy with the lady in red to notice as I circle around.

According to the map, somewhere nearby is the kitchen. I spot a set of swinging doors with waiters passing in and out. Phew. According to the map, just inside those doors is a hallway leading to the back stairs. At the top is Mohammad's office.

I take a deep breath and slip inside the enormous kitchen, bustling with servers and cooks. Before anyone notices, I duck into the hallway. It's empty, probably because every single servant and then some are on duty. I look back, making sure I'm not followed. Then I run to the stairway. With a thud, I bump into Cintia, floating down the steps in a flowing white gown like a Grecian goddess.

"Jenna. What on earth are you doing here?"

Oh great. Now what?

"Cintia. Hi! I was looking for a restroom."

Her eyes narrow. Is she suspicious? What does she think, I'm going to steal something?

Oh yeah, I am.

"You know. Girl time?" I pat my tummy as if to say it's my time of the month. "I was hoping to find you or Fatima or one of the private bathrooms..."

Her face softens. "Ah. I understand. Come with me. There's bound to be a wait on the ground floor. It will be faster to go upstairs."

She leads me up the narrow stairs to her third-floor suite of rooms, stopping in front of the door to her office.

"Isn't the restroom that way?" I point down the hallway.

"I keep feminine things in the spare bathroom," she explains, smiling.

As she reaches for the door handle, a silver ring catches my eye. Something about the ring is familiar. I try to get a closer look, but Cintia has already stepped into the room. That's strange. I stand outside the doorway, hesitant to walk through. Something feels wrong. It's probably just my fear of snakes bothering me.

"Come now, Jenna." Cintia interrupts my thoughts. "I have everything you need."

I step inside.

Chapter 29
Scheherazade

The glass wall of reptile terrariums casts an eerie orange glow. Cintia points to a door I hadn't noticed last time we were here. Her desk is covered in swatches of paper and fashionable-magazines. I try not to disturb anything with my flouncy skirt as I step into the bathroom.

Once inside, I open drawers and cabinets, looking for a tampon. I use up the appropriate amount of time, punctuated with the sounds of tearing paper, running water, and flushing toilet. Now I need to find a way to get past Cintia and into Mohammad's office.

When I exit, Cintia is standing in front of the terrariums, admiring her beloved pets. The heat lamps illuminate her face. She taps a blood-red nail against the glass, then turns to me.

"That is such a beautiful dress, Jenna. And so becoming on you. Come closer." I set my jeweled clutch down on the desk and reluctantly cross the room. "Where did you find it?" she asks.

"Actually, I'm not sure. It arrived today. I thought maybe the sheik sent it? Or you and Fatima? To make sure I'd arrive looking presentable?"

Cintia tilts her head curiously. "Oh, Jenna. We don't judge by appearances. Perhaps one of your admirers sent it?"

"Admirers?" I laugh at the thought of having admirers.

"You are so unaware of your powers, dear." She waves her hand in the air, dismissing my statement. "I noticed it at tea with Evan. In my country we have a saying, *Al Aleb Ghaleb.* 'You are more lovely than your dress.' And so you are. Men find you intriguing, Jenna."

I blush, uncertain how to respond. Cintia runs her hand along the smooth glass until she comes to the cage of the largest snake. She carefully lifts the lid, cooing at the hideous slithering beast inside. I steady myself on the edge of the couch, trying to hide my revulsion.

Cintia slips a hand in and slowly pulls out a snake at least five feet long. It has a purple and brown geometric pattern broken up by pale rectangles. On a Bedouin textile, the design would be beautiful. In this situation, it's impossible to get past the scales. She strokes the snake's back.

I notice her ring again. It has a familiar shape—two crossed swords with an eye. The center is made of black onyx. Where have I seen that image?

As she walks toward me with the enormous reptile, the hair pricks up on the back of my neck. Has she forgotten I'm not exactly a fan of snakes?

"May I ask where you got that ring?"

"This? It's been in my family for years. It was handed down to me. I've actually never worn it before. But tonight is a special occasion."

"The design is so unusual."

"What a shame you don't appreciate snakes, Jenna. There are

so many things to admire about them. Their patience, their adaptability. Snakes are some of the oldest inhabitants of our planet."

The snake's silver eyes flick back and forth. I don't know much about reptiles, but this one has a wide head and is eerily motionless.

"Does he have a name?" I ask, forcibly repressing a scream.

"*She*. Her name is Scheherazade, after the queen who sacrificed herself and married the Sultan to stop him killing innocents."

There is something particularly ominous about Scheherazade's head, thick and boney with a black line dividing the skull and two thick black triangles on her cheeks. She watches me, very still, almost sluggish.

"Perhaps if you spent more time with reptiles, you could overcome your fear."

Cintia steps forward, so close I can feel her breath, then slowly drapes the snake over my shoulders. At that exact moment, I realize where I've seen the ring—The Weavers of the Desert exhibit at the museum.

It's the Zahar crest.

Cintia looks at me with her perfect almond eyes. We share a moment of recognition. The ring bears the mark of the Bedouins which can mean only one thing—Cintia is a member of the Zahar tribe.

I freeze, panic rising. My breath stops. How can that be? Does that mean she's involved somehow? I need to get out of here.

"Um, she's heavy," I say, feeling the weight and thickness of the snake's body. The tail coils over my right arm, and her head rests over my heart, tongue flicking against my skin. Tonight has officially turned into my worst nightmare. I try not to show my fear, but perspiration is breaking out on my forehead.

"Do you recognize the pattern?"

I close my eyes and take a breath, trying to master my fear, not only of the snake, but the newly discovered predator in the room.

"Snakes are not my forte," I whisper through gritted teeth. "A boa constrictor?"

Cintia shakes her head.

"Python?"

"Not exactly." Cynthia smiles, and there is something sad about her smile. Something regretful. "This snake is considerably more rare."

I try not to move as I glance at the snake. The pattern is unusual—there are those odd little horns by her nostrils. What did I read about snakes with horns?

"Give up?"

I nod. Cintia strokes the snake and says coolly, "Scheherazade is a Gaboon viper."

My breath catches in my lungs. "A viper?"

I know boa constrictors and pythons kill by squeezing their prey to death. Vipers bite, injecting venom. My muscles tighten as a shot of fear rushes through my veins.

"I wouldn't move if I were you, Jenna. She has the largest venom sack in the world—the longest fangs. Don't let her stillness fool you. She can strike at any moment. When she does, her speed is shocking, and she won't let go until you die. A single drop of her venom is deadly."

My muscles twitch involuntarily.

"Oh careful, dear. It's really sudden movements she hates most."

I take a slow breath, trying to stay calm.

"Why are you doing this?" I whisper.

"You're a bright girl. If you've connected my ring to my tribe, you'll figure the rest out soon enough. And I can't risk you or anyone else stopping me."

The viper lifts its head slightly. I try to remain absolutely still.

"If you're a member of the Zahar tribe, why would the sheik marry you?"

"When Mohammad met me, I went by my grandmother's name, Saleh. He had no idea he was marrying the daughter of Hussein Khalid."

A tiny shiver of fear moves through me, and the snake swells in response. A low growling hiss rises from Scheherazade's throat.

"Do you hear that, Jenna?" Cintia smiles lovingly. "Such a wondrous creature. She's considering whether or not to strike."

Tears well up in my eyes, but I can't afford to lose my composure. The animal can feel everything. I force myself to breathe slowly and evenly.

"I saw a girl die from Gaboon venom once." Cintia's eyes grow distant as she remembers the scene. "Within fifteen minutes, she was bleeding from every orifice."

Oh no! This is how Adar Abassi died. Hemorrhaging.

Images of Abassi dying flood my mind. The snake stirs and adjusts herself, coiling around my shoulders in a lazy circle. I take a slow calming breath and ask, "Why did you kill Adar Abassi?"

She nods as if my question is reasonable, even expected. "Adar was my cousin. We spent our lives preparing for vengeance. But he grew soft. He wanted to abandon our plan. I had no choice. It took only the prick of a needle dipped in venom to silence him."

"Adar was a Zahar? But I thought he hated Bedouins?"

She shrugs. "He was a good actor, but perhaps there was a bit of self-loathing."

"And Evan?"

"Oh poor, dumb Evan. Vengeance does not come cheap, Jenna. I've been sending money home, in various ways, for years. Evan literally stumbled on an account he wasn't meant to see. He began to ask questions. And he and my cousin were so close. I feared Adar, in his effort to stop me, would confide in Evan."

"So you're the one paying Ali Kabir?"

"Yes. Occasionally, over the years, I would send papers, information, money home through Adar. Always the helpful wife, I often made deliveries to Evan for Mohammad."

"You ordered the hit on Evan and Adar?"

"My plan was quite simple. Stage a mugging with the payment for the hitmen, hidden in the lining of the stolen briefcase. I only had to sneak into Mohammad's office and get the money in the case before it was sealed. Both Evan and Adar would have been eliminated in one, tragic New York crime. Had you not interrupted, my plan would have been perfect."

"And now you mean to kill Mohammad? All because he's the son of the man who killed your father? What about Fatima? I saw you together. You love her. You can't fake that."

Cintia clenches her fists, eyes blazing. "I am the daughter of Hussein Khalid. The Zahar are my family. Our blood demands retribution."

"But this is your family now, Cintia. Mohammad, Fatima, even Evan. They trust you."

"My father was condemned to death by Faisal Ab El Malik and beheaded like a dog in the city square. I watched him die. Do you have any idea how that feels?"

"No, of course not. But—"

"Ali Kabir raised me. He trained me, sent me to schools where I would be educated and connect with these people. He shaped me into an instrument of death and seduction. I am the weapon that will avenge my father. It is my fate." She speaks clearly and proudly, as if she has been practicing this speech her whole life.

"There is still time to stop this. The FBI are watching. They know the mugging was suspicious. They'll catch you."

"Catch me?" Cintia laughs. "My entire existence has led to this moment, Jenna. I don't plan on escaping. When all eyes are on my husband, I will avenge my father's death. Then my life will be complete."

Cintia walks to her desk and removes a velvet box from the bottom drawer. She extracts a curved silver knife, its blade coated with a thick, milky crust.

"In their war with Alexander the Great, the Indians used blood and dung to thicken the poison. I've changed the recipe, but the main ingredient is still poison. In this case, my lovely Scheherazade's venom." She looks fondly at the snake weighing heavy on my shoulders.

Cintia holds the knife up to the light. "This blade belonged to my father." She looks at me. "It is better to die in revenge, than to live in shame."

She tucks the knife into the folds of her gown and walks to the door. "Don't worry. Scheherazade has plenty of venom left for you. As I said, it only takes a drop. I'll leave you to your fate now. Mine awaits downstairs." She smiles at me serenely as if all is right in the world, then switches off the light, slips out of the room, and closes the door.

In the darkness, Scheherazade sinks her body deeper into the warm curve of my neck. I empty my mind, trying to release all thoughts, all fear. I tense my bicep, preparing to lift her slowly, but the snake puffs her body up and begins a low, warning hiss.

Maybe, if I shift infinitesimally and lower my left side a little, gravity will gently draw her head down. I lean my weight back against the couch, allowing my shoulder to drop the tiniest bit. Her scales fan over my heart, then she begins to slither down, sensing the flow of gravity until her head is touching my lap. I think my idea is working when Scheherazade stops, content to rest her huge head on my thigh.

In the darkness, I can feel the weight of her and her deep stillness. My arms and legs are numb, but I've managed to extend my breath so I'm barely expanding my ribcage. I try to pretend the snake is Max, sleeping on my lap, and I don't want to disturb him.

I worry someone will walk in, startle the big snake, and she'll bite. No. There's little chance of that or Cintia wouldn't have risked leaving me here. All I can do is wait, and hope the snake moves on her own. I can't think bad thoughts. She'll sense it.

Finally, after what seems like an unbearable length of time, Scheherazade's head slides further down my thigh, then curves around my calf. I am literally engulfed by her body, but the most important part, the most dangerous part of her, the fangs, are moving toward the floor. I barely breathe as her great triangular head slides along my ankle and over my foot, followed by her heavy, cold body.

I can't see where Scheherazade has gone in the darkness. It's a risk to move, but I have to get out of this room. How long have I been in here? The sheik could be dead by now. I'm stiff from holding still for so long and anxious to alert the sheik. But if I move suddenly and she's within reach, the snake will strike, and this will have all been for nothing. *Do not blow this, Jenna.*

Slowly, I pluck my way over the couch and onto a chair before letting my feet touch the ground. I squeeze past the desk, holding my breath, praying the sheik is still alive. I've got to warn him.

As I open the door, the light from the hallway floods inside. I look back and catch a glimpse of the viper, curled up underneath the couch in a mound of beautifully patterned death.

Chapter 30
Cold Blooded

I'm leaning against the doorway, catching my breath, when it hits me. I left Dave's clutch behind. What's worse? The wrath of Dave or Scheherazade? It's a toss-up. I crack the door. The viper is exactly where I left her, napping or whatever it is snakes do. I hold my breath, snatch the bag from the corner of the desk, and shut the door firmly. This silly little clutch better be worth a lot of money!

I pull out my phone and check the time. Over an hour since we first arrived. That means I must have been in the room with that creature on my shoulders for at least thirty minutes. No wonder it seemed like an eternity. It was.

I abandon my treacherous shoes and rush down the back stairs to the second floor. The hallway is empty. I hurry past silent doorways. Ahead is the grand staircase. I lean on the banister and assess the situation. The cocktail party is over, the screens have been moved aside, and the banquet is just starting. Dinner guests are seated, chatting and drinking while the wait staff delivers the salad course.

The sheik is seated at the head table, flanked by his two wives, Fatima and Cintia. He has a commanding view of the room. Cintia hasn't made her move yet. What is she waiting for?

For a moment, I watch her, fascinated. She is the consummate hostess, laughing, enjoying herself. She's absolutely charming. She touches the sheik's hand lightly, and Fatima smiles at her with affection. Everyone is completely fooled. I want to shout and warn them, but Cintia is within striking range. If I threaten her vengeance, she might speed up her plan.

What should I do? Evan is seated on the other side of Fatima next to my empty chair. He keeps looking around for me, as if he's worried, but obviously not worried enough to come look for me. Jerk! I could call him. Hopefully he would answer the phone. But asking him to disarm a psychotic killer? His self-conscious behavior doesn't exactly inspire confidence.

I could call Denning or Cole or Wolfson, or a bomb threat into 911. But no matter what I do, Cintia will have plenty of time to thrust the knife into her unsuspecting husband. And it only takes one drop of venom to kill.

As I consider my options, Cintia notices me. An expression of surprise momentarily disrupts her mask of composure. Then without any fear or emotion, she signals someone across the room with a nod.

I follow her gaze, and my breath catches in my throat. Sasha Kurgan is standing at the bottom of the staircase, dressed in formal attire. He looks up at me, and his brow darkens. He nods at Cintia and takes the stairs two at a time.

Are you kidding me?

He's almost at the landing when I run. After twenty-five feet, he's closing in on me. I'll never make it to the back stairway. The door to my right is locked, but the one on my left opens. I run through a labyrinth of offices and meeting rooms.

Behind me, Kurgan starts growling. "Little bird? Where are you?"

Oh great. I guess that makes him the cat.

Finally, I emerge into the sheik's large, empty office. How ironic. No time to download your files now, Cole. Besides, I already know who the bad guy—I mean girl—happens to be.

My heart beats fast as I slip through the maze of rooms, following the map in my head, working my way in a circle. I need to slow Kurgan down. I reach a heavy door and wait until he steps into the room. He rushes toward me, enraged. Before he can reach me, I slam the door and latch it. He rattles the handle in frustration. I run into the hallway, but Kurgan is faster than I thought, bursting into the space between me and the grand stairway.

I have no choice. I sprint for the back stairs.

Kurgan's footsteps are loud as he closes the distance. I push through the door, then hesitate. I'll never make it to the kitchen, but I have an idea. I gather up the layers of my skirt and climb to the third floor.

Kurgan is behind me, boots heavy on the steps, grunting with effort. I run to Cintia's office, out of breath, and open the door.

It takes a moment for my eyes to adjust to the darkness. Then I see her. Scheherazade hasn't moved. She's coiled in the shadows, absolutely still. I empty my mind and try to imagine the snake as my friend, here to help me.

Carefully, I slide to the far side of the desk, as close to Scheherazade as I dare. No sudden moves. Then I wait, catching my breath.

Sasha Kurgan appears, backlit in the doorway. "Now I've got you," he growls and steps into the room, face twisted in anger, thick jaw forming a wretched grin. He sees me in the shadows and stops to evaluate the situation. Realizing I'm unarmed, his smile widens, and he closes the door. Now, the only light is the orange glow of the terrariums.

"Stupid girl, you trap yourself."

"Listen Sasha, back off slowly, or I'll be forced to kill you."

With a huff of disdain, Kurgan pulls a razor wire out of his pocket. With a hiss, the wire stretches between the length of his hands. Sergei's words come into my mind—Sasha Kurgan doesn't need a gun to kill.

"You? Kill me?" Laughter erupts from his heavy frame as he lumbers toward me. "A stupid little girl like you?"

"I'm warning you." I hold my breath, keeping absolutely still.

He laughs again. Out of the corner of my eye, I see Scheherazade's dark head lift, startled by the sound.

"You are the one who dies tonight, and with great pain. Gun too noisy, too much blood. But wire will suffocate you, no screaming, just pain."

Kurgan steps across the thick white carpet, holding up the razor wire. He lunges toward me. But I'm ready. I roll under him as he charges. Then I push up with all of my strength, directing his heavy body across the desk. The messy surface aids his momentum, and he slides across, scattering stacks of paper and magazines, before toppling over and landing hard on the floor—right next to the viper.

There's a low growl and a hiss as Scheherazade strikes, slicing into Kurgan's leg with her two-inch-long fangs. He looks at me, surprised, then tries to struggle to his feet, kicking his leg violently, to shake off the snake. But the viper only grips harder. The razor wire drops from his hands. He tries to grab the snake's tail, but Scheherazade is pure muscle.

"What have you done? You bitch!" he screams, falling back against the couch, confused, in shock. The venom works fast. Blood begins to stream from his nose. He holds his hands up to his face and catches the drops as they splatter onto his palms. Blood pours from his lower lip, down the front of his shirt, until a wide, red stain covers the place where his heart should be.

"I eat little girls like you for breakfast," he chokes out, speech garbled. He reaches for me, but he can't see. His tissue is swelling up, blistering. He's blind.

"Not anymore," I whisper, backing up against the door.

He tries to climb across the couch as the poison breaks down his tissue. Blood smears the white cushions.

I can't watch anymore. As I start to back out of the room, the lights flick on. Cole Braedon steps into the room, eyes narrow, taking in the dying man, the viper latched onto his leg.

Kurgan tries to hoist himself up on the couch, then tumbles to the floor again, smearing blood across the couch and rug.

Cole hands me my silver shoes. "You forgot these," he says calmly.

Now he shows up? Cole really needs to work on his timing. I wish he had shown up an hour ago. He probably wouldn't have even been scared. I slip my shoes back on, trying not to throw up.

Cole calmly walks across the room and gently grabs the snake. He slides his hand up the length of her body and presses the hinge of her jaw, forcing her mouth open. He unhooks her fangs and walks her slowly back to the terrarium, where he picks up a wrangling stick and secures her head. Then he releases Scheherazade back into her home. I hear him whisper quietly under his breath.

"What a good snake you are."

Kurgan lies in a deepening pool of blood, eyes wide open, staring into the distance.

"Shouldn't we call an ambulance?"

"He's dead, Jenna. And even if he wasn't, there's no antivenin for Gaboon viper in New York City."

Well, that figures. Cole Braedon recognizes the actual species.

This is the second death I've witnessed this week. I felt sad for Adar Abassi. His death seemed wrong. This time all I feel is relief. No regret. No sorrow. No fear. Just overwhelming relief.

"Is there some reason you know how to handle poisonous snakes, Cole? I mean, does that come up a lot in your line of work?"

"More than you'd think. You'd be surprised how many criminals just *love* their pet snakes."

Cole searches Kurgan, then pockets his gun, wallet, and phone. To him, it's nothing. Dead guy on the floor. Next.

At least the idea of touching a dead body disturbs me. Is Cole's level of detachment what I have to look forward to? He brushes off his hands as if you can wipe death away. He's so casual about it all.

"I don't want to be like you," flies out of my mouth without thinking.

"No, you don't," he agrees, unfazed by my declaration. Cole shakes his head in wonder and looks at me curiously. "Do you want to tell me how the hell you ended up taking out a trained Krov hitman with a Gaboon viper? Here I thought you needed my help."

"Look, right now we have a bigger problem. Cintia has a knife coated with" —I point toward the terrarium— "that."

"*That,* as in *venom?*"

"Yes. She plans to kill the sheik."

"Why?" Cole's face darkens like a storm.

"A blood feud. The sheik's father executed her father. Ali Kabir raised her to be an assassin. The whole thing, the marriage, her whole life, has led up to this one goal. She's finishing it, avenging her father's death—tonight."

"Come on." Cole grabs my arm abruptly and pulls me out of the room. He moves through the house as if he has the layout memorized, rushing down the back staircase, past the kitchen, and through a set of French doors. We end up in a darkened alcove.

From our hiding place, the sheik's table is visible. Fatima gently taps on a water glass and the dinner guests quiet down. Some begin to playfully chime their own glasses.

"And now my husband would like to say a few words," Fatima says.

"Speech, speech!" call a few of the guests.

I squeeze Cole's arm, remembering what Cintia said when she was trying to kill me.

"When we were upstairs," I whisper to him, "Cintia said she would avenge her father's death when all eyes were on her husband. She knew he'd be making a speech. What are we going to do?"

"Hold on, I've got an idea," Cole says. He pulls Kurgan's phone out of his pocket and scrolls through the numbers. His fingers move quickly, typing out a text. "Let's see if we can get her away from him."

Cintia's phone vibrates, and she looks down at her lap. Abruptly, she stands up and politely makes her excuses. Then she walks out of the banquet area and through the ballroom toward the large exit doors.

"What did you say?"

"That he needs to see her in the kitchen urgently. Or her mission will fail."

Cole grabs my shoulders and looks deep into my eyes. He brushes the hair from my face and straightens out the fabric of my dress.

"Listen, I need you to warn the sheik and Fatima. Whatever it takes, get them out of here. Now."

"What about you?"

"I'm going to grab Cintia."

I nod gravely. It hits me. There's no antivenin in New York City. As Cole turns to walk away, a wave of anxiety flows over me. Not for me, but for him. He's about to confront a murderer with a poisoned dagger. After what happened to Sasha Kurgan, I realize this situation is deadly.

"Cole!" He looks back at me.

"The knife is in the folds of her dress, tucked into her belt. Don't let her cut you. She'll do anything to avenge her father. Be careful."

He looks back at me and smiles.

"Always."

Chapter 31
The Sand Beneath My Skin

Cintia glides past the alcove, heading toward her rendezvous. As soon as she's gone, I walk between the open screens, heading for the sheik's table. So much for my Cinderella moment. This evening has taken a deadly turn.

Evan spots me and frowns. Then he taps his watch, embarrassed by my late appearance. Excuse me if I was busy fighting off —not one, but two—murderers. I glare at him, trying to express how angry I am he didn't come looking for me. But he's not getting the message. He just looks tense and confused. How can he be so thick?

Mohammad and Fatima are laughing and enjoying themselves. They must be waiting for Cintia to return before the sheik begins his speech. To Evan's horror, instead of going to him, I walk around the edge of the table. My plan is to quietly explain to Mohammad and Fatima that we all need to exit the room.

But what do I say? How do I get them to leave? Telling the truth will take too long and would they even believe me? Probably not. They might even refuse to go.

I'm almost at the head of the table when I catch a flutter of white out of the corner of my eye. Cintia is back, heading quickly toward the sheik, her long gown floating as if made of spun sugar.

How did she get away from Cole Braedon? Something obviously went wrong. I scan the edges of the room searching for him. Then, across the ballroom, Cole steps out of the shadows and signals, warning me to withdraw.

But I can't do that—I'm on my own.

As Cintia sweeps up to the table, there's only one move left. I take a deep breath and stand between her and Mohammad.

Cintia stops barely two feet in front of me. She isn't ready to give it up, but the time for niceties is over.

"Jenna, how nice of you to join us. May I take my seat please?"

"I don't think that's a good idea." I stand frozen.

The diners look up at Cintia and me, causing a scene. An anxious murmur ripples through the room. Who is this crazy girl disturbing our exclusive dinner?

"Excuse me, *Jenna*, but Mohammad is about to speak," Cintia says as calmly as if I accidentally went for the wrong chair.

"I won't let you kill him," I tell her sternly.

Fatima and a few ladies at the table gasp, while the men stare at me in outrage. I am violating all of their rules. A flurry of whispers circulates. Then Mohammad stands up with a swirl of his robes.

"What is this nonsense?" He throws down his napkin.

Fatima looks at Evan for an explanation.

"Jenna! What are you doing?" Evan chokes, pointing frantically to the chair beside him, indicating I should sit down and be quiet. His face is drained of color. He's mortified.

Cintia waves to the two closest security guards, who are watching us intently. They move forward to remove me.

Then Cintia's tapered fingers grip the hilt of the dagger hidden in her dress. She takes a step closer, eyes locked on Mohammad.

"I know you think you have to do this," I say to her, "but you don't. If people have the will, they can control their destinies."

She smiles at my use of the familiar Bedouin saying. "That is a quaint proverb. But we have another. 'At the narrow passage, there is no brother and no friend.'"

"Jenna, this is ridiculous. What's going on?" Evan rises from his seat warily. The way Cintia and I are quoting Bedouin sayings is no doubt confusing to him. Time to pour some gasoline on that fire.

"Evan, let me introduce you to the daughter of Hussein Khalid, sworn enemy of the Ab El Maliks." A sudden, ominous silence cloaks the room, followed by shocked voices.

"*Khalid?* That is not possible." Mohammad strikes his own palm definitively.

"Lies!" Fatima says, getting to her feet.

"Is this a joke, Jenna? Why would you say something so... crazy?" Evan asks miserably.

The security guards are almost at the table. If they grab me, Cintia will stab Mohammad in a heartbeat. I hold my hands up, blocking her access to the sheik.

"Because it's true." I speak loudly so everyone can hear. "Cintia is here to settle a blood feud—for the Zahar."

"The tribe responsible for my elder brother's death?" Mohammad shakes his head. "No, this cannot be."

"It's true. Hussein Khalid was executed by your father. Now the Zahar want revenge."

Evan looks like he is about to faint. Another murmur sweeps through the crowd.

"Why do you speak these lies?" The sheik says in a warning voice. "Khalid was a traitor."

Cintia is rigid, eyes black with hatred. It shouldn't take much to push her now.

"Well, Cintia? Was your father a traitor? Will you defend him?"

Her eyes flash and her mask drops away.

"My father was no traitor. He was loyal. He knew nothing of the plot to kill your brother!"

The sheik's eyes widen. The security guards stop, realizing something is wrong.

"It is not possible." Fatima puts a hand over her heart. "You? My dear one?"

"Believe it, my sister. It is the truth." Cintia's eyes fill with tears and her lip trembles. Slowly, she draws the dagger out of the folds of her gown. Light reflects off the handle and sparks along the curving blade dipped in poison.

Fatima shrieks. The sheik thrusts his arm across her chest, like a parent protecting a child in a car crash. I puff up and stand tall, blocking Cintia's access to the sheik with my body.

There is a strange moment of affinity between Cintia and me. Our paths are chosen. We are both locked in now—to the death.

Cintia quickly presses the flat edge of the blade against my throat. I stand still, afraid to move, knowing the deadly poison is on the knife. She pulls me against her and turns me around, using me as a human shield. People gasp in horror. A woman cries out. Some of the guests begin to flee.

"Tell your men to move back, or she dies."

I stand completely still. The musky smell of venom rises up from the blade to my nose. It smells like death and betrayal. The sheik waves his security men back.

"Do as she commands." His expression has crumpled into a deep sadness.

Cintia holds me tight as she inches toward Mohammad. Her breath is erratic. She's trying to hold back tears. Now that the moment has arrived, she's torn. She doesn't want to do this. It's a duty, not a choice.

Cole makes his way toward me, frustrated and angry, but still too far away to help. Evan is frozen in shock and horror. Finally, he seems to understand what's happening.

I only have one weapon—that Cintia is torn.

"Fatima deserves to know why you plan to kill her husband," I manage to choke out.

"Quiet," Cintia hisses.

Fatima sobs with complete abandon. She looks at Cintia and cries out, "Please, sister. Are we not family?"

Cintia keeps the knife on my throat as she speaks. "My father was beheaded like a dog. My family lives in shame in a garbage dump."

Fatima wails. I feel Cintia's body shudder. She is shaking, growing more conflicted. The blade dances dangerously against my throat in her uncertain hand.

"Please, Cintia," I plead. "They know only what they were told —just like you. Mohammad is innocent. He didn't order your father's death. They are your family now."

Cintia remains quiet.

"I know you love them!" I gasp.

"That is my misfortune," Cintia finally responds. "Mohammad is his father's son, as I am my father's daughter. His father commanded the death of mine. Nothing can change my destiny."

Tears stream down Cintia's face. Determined, she raises her hand to lunge at the sheik.

Fatima screams. That's all I need—I elbow Cintia in the ribs. She pitches forward, gasping for breath. Then I strike her wrist with the heavy, jeweled bag. The dagger falls to the ground. Cintia drops to her knees, disoriented from the blows. She picks up the knife and the security men rush forward, but the sheik raises his hand to stop them.

"Dear one," the sheik implores her. "I do not care about blood feuds. Those are the old ways. We can take this horror and use it for good, unite our families, work together for progress." He reaches for Cintia, his face wracked with grief.

On her hands and knees on the floor, Cintia's back rises and falls as she breathes deeply, slowing her tears, calming herself. For a moment, the crisis seems to be over. Cintia seems so still, willing to give up, to heed the sheik's words. The entire room is frozen in anticipation. Mohammad raises his hand again, letting everyone know to give her a moment to collect herself.

Finally, Cintia looks up at the sheik. She extends the knife toward him, handle first, in surrender. As he reaches to take it, she says sadly, "I cannot live without honor." With a powerful thrust, she plunges the dagger deep into her own heart.

Fatima shrieks and falls to her knees.

The sheik, his face in anguish, kneels down and pulls Cintia into his arms as the fast-acting venom takes hold.

"Call an ambulance!" he cries out as his security men scatter to get help.

"The knife is poisoned with venom," I whisper. "There's no antidote."

Mohammad nods as tears cascade down his cheeks. He looks down at his dying wife. "I did not know how much suffering my father caused. I would have tried to make amends. This should never have come to pass." The sheik cradles Cintia's head against his chest. She reaches up and touches his cheek gently.

"I am so sorry, my love," she says, then reaches toward Fatima. "Sister—"

Rendered awkward by her deep sobs, Fatima crawls to Cintia's side. She takes Cintia's hand and kisses it as blood begins to trickle from the younger woman's nose.

Mohammad continues, his voice growing strong with resolve. "I promise to restore the honor of your people. No Khalid will ever live in shame again. Our families will be at peace. Your death will not be in vain."

Blood pours from Cintia's nose and mouth, staining the sheik's white robes.

"I feel the sand... beneath my skin," she smiles weakly. "You honor me."

As Cintia shudders into death, the sheik rocks her in his arms and weeps.

Chapter 32
Guilty Pleasure

The mansion is bathed in the glow of red and blue police lights. The sirens have stopped blaring, and I've already given my formal statement. I'm waiting for the okay to leave. But I had to get out of that house.

I sink back against one of the stone columns, rubbing my neck. I'm going to be sore tomorrow.

Across from me, leaning on the other column, is Cole Braedon, smoking a black cigarette with a gold filter and a crown emblem. He takes a drag and offers me one from a pack wrapped in gold foil.

"No thanks. What brand is that?" I envy him. He's the kind of person who can smoke and not think about lung cancer.

"An expensive one. My guilty pleasure."

The scent is spicy, strangely aromatic, and the night breeze feels good on my skin as I lean against the cool stone. Up above heavy clouds roll to the east. The air feels wet, threatening rain.

A comfortable silence falls between us. Right now, Cole is the one person in the world who understands what really happened in there.

Guests trickle out into the night as the police release them. A few appear shocked. Others seem genuinely shattered. A husband folds his coat around his wife, who is wiping away tears. So many lives affected.

A second CSI unit arrives, and more people in blue windbreakers hurry up the steps and into the mansion. The lights on the cop cars and a lone, unnecessary ambulance cast strange, unsteady shadows. Attendants carry a gurney down the steps with a body zipped up in a bag.

"That would be Sasha Kurgan, headed for the morgue," Cole observes offhandedly. He releases a cloud of smoke into the air and puts his cigarette out on the ground.

Then he slides next to me, so close I can feel the heat from his body.

"How do you feel?"

"You mean after being an integral part in the deaths of two people? Not great."

"You only helped Kurgan along. Besides, he deserved it."

"Even if he was scum, I still led him to the jaws of a viper."

"Kurgan was an assassin, Jenna. Killing him was self-defense. You get that, right?"

I shrug and look up at the stormy sky.

"And you saved the sheik," he adds. "That speech you made turned everything around. Wolfson is going to be proud of you."

I don't know what to say to that. The adrenaline has finally worn off. All that's left now is exhaustion. I'm beyond crying, but even if I could manage a tear, I'm not about to cry in front of Cole.

"So what happened in there, anyway? I saw Cintia heading your way..."

Cole shakes his head. "Our eyes met, and somehow Cintia

knew. Before I could get to her, she turned around and headed for you."

"I guess everyone's got a plan until they get punched," I say, quoting Mike Tyson.

Cole laughs. "True. What about you?" he asks. "When did you know Cintia was behind everything?"

"I recognized the crest of the Zahar tribe on her ring. By then it was too late. She had me alone with Scheherazade. Even then, part of me didn't want to believe it."

Cole folds his hands thoughtfully.

"The first few times an adversary makes the decision to kill you, it's hard to believe. Later, you come to expect it."

"I don't want to come to expect it! No one ever tried to kill me before! People are basically good, Cole."

He smirks and shoves his hands in his pockets. He's pulled his tie loose and his dark hair falls over his eyes.

"A wise detective is realistic about people."

"By realistic you mean suspicious?"

"Is there a difference?"

I look at him, perplexed. Does he really believe that? He stares back blankly.

"That moment, when everything sharpens. When you see behind the curtain and know what you have to do. That moment is more important than preserving some childish idea of how life should be, Jenna. Better to lose your innocence than your life."

"Wolfson says I have a Pandora instinct. Now I think I understand. Pandora left hope in the box because it was the last shred of innocence that makes life worth living."

"Every case will have a moment that draws on all of your skills and knowledge to reveal the truth. That's a moment worth living for. Never ignore your instincts, Jenna. That's what will keep you, and those who rely on you, alive when nothing else can." Cole reaches over and tips my chin up, so I'm looking into his deep green eyes. For a moment, I feel myself falling, the world dissolving around us. The way he looks at me, it's as if he can see all the hidden twists and turns of my soul.

"You did good, Jenna Stack."

He leans toward me. A shock of electricity runs through me and air rushes into my lungs. But instead of kissing me, he runs a thumb over my mouth, wiping something away.

"Blood. It's gone now."

Blood? Gross!

Cole reaches over and smooths the upturned sleeve of my dress.

"You do look beautiful. I knew that color would suit you."

My mouth opens in shock. "*You?* You sent the dress?"

He shrugs.

"A couture dress? Really? How on earth did you get your hands on something like this?"

He smiles a self-satisfied grin, enjoying the fact I've underestimated him yet again. Who is this guy, and why do I always feel like I'm a step behind him?

"Did you know about the viper too?"

"Come on, Jenna. I know you think I'm trouble, but do you really think I'd risk your life?"

"Good question."

He's been working awfully hard to keep me alive, but that was when he needed me. Would he let me die if I wasn't going to be useful? I honestly don't know.

Cole turns suddenly, tilting his head to one side like a wolf listening to something we humans can't hear.

"I have to go now. See you around."

"Not in a surveillance van, I hope."

But he's gone. I'm standing alone, considering the exchange, when a deep, masculine voice says, "Did I hear you talking to someone?"

I turn and see Detective John Denning, wearing a leather jacket and jeans, walking toward me with that restless energy.

"No one important," I say and face him.

He looks me up and down in my party dress, trying not to appear shocked. I'm starting to wonder what I usually look like to people.

"You clean up pretty good. Exciting night?"

"You might say that. Do I need to come down to the station?"

He shakes his head. "We've got your statement. And there are a hundred witnesses who saw what happened tonight."

"Good. Dave went home after cocktails and missed all the action. Have I got a story for him."

Denning bends down and picks up something from the floor— a black cigarette butt with a gold filter. He turns it in his hand until he sees the crown emblem.

"This may be an empty gesture, but I'm going to give you a little free advice," he says gruffly. "Next time you see trouble coming, step out of the way. That includes getting involved with questionable men."

"You mean like Cole Braedon?" I can't resist tormenting Denning ever so slightly.

"Exactly," Denning says, his handsome face clouding over. He has a boyish quality, a note of sadness in those clear blue eyes. "Anyway, I'm glad you're safe."

"Thanks, I've had enough trouble."

"Good." Denning seems to want to say more, then thinks better of it. "Goodnight, Miss Stack."

At that moment, the sheik's white limo pulls up. Evan waves me over. I guess it's time for Cinderella to catch a ride home.

"Goodnight," I say. But Denning's already disappeared inside the mansion.

~

I lean my head back on the plush leather seat, allowing the steady movement of the limo to rock me as I watch the city blur past. There's a feeling of vibrancy in the air, electricity. The city streets look beautiful in the cool, misty air.

I know from working with therapy groups at Bellevue, I've probably got a touch of PTSD, caused by witnessing so much violence. I counseled enough people about the effects: heightened senses, intrusive recollections, distressing dreams, arousal. What if I had killed someone directly? How much worse would it be?

Looking over at Evan, I'm worried. There's a haunted look in his eyes. He's taken off his jacket and bowtie, loosened his collar, and untucked his shirt. I've never seen him look so disheveled, even when he was wearing that pink robe.

Observing him, I'm aware he's only comfortable, only powerful, with a managed form of reality: lists, schedules, structure. He doesn't do well with chaos. He has the window half-rolled down and is drinking in the cool air. Sweat has soaked through his dress shirt and his cheeks are flushed. He's been like this for ten minutes.

"Are you sure you're all right?" I ask gently. When he turns to look at me, there's a mixture of fear and horror in his expression. He's wound so tight, I'm almost afraid to disturb him, for fear he'll implode.

"How do you do it, Jenna? How do you stay so calm? I've never watched a person die before. It was so damn awful, like that scene in *Apocalypse Now*. You know, where they sacrifice the cow with a sword?"

Okay, well that's pretty Freudian, and dramatic. But it's a fair question.

"Evan, you're in shock. Cintia was your friend, but she was also a *fanatic*. She fooled everyone, even her own husband. She hired a hitman to kill you, poisoned Abassi, and had a knife to my throat. It's okay to mourn her, but there was no saving her."

"You're right." He shakes his head. "It's just... so... *awful*." Evan sinks against me, burying his face in my hair. I put my arms around him. There's nothing I can do to wipe the image of Cintia dying from his mind, or from my own. All I can do is try to console him.

The limo driver, an expert in human behavior, discreetly raises the privacy glass. We're left in a bubble of luxury and sadness, each struggling to process the horrible events of the evening.

"Even though she did those awful things, you saw her face. She cared about her family. She cared about you."

I feel him nod his head slightly.

"In the end, she chose to die. And that's on her. You're going to have to find a way to let her go and live with it."

Evan looks up at me, his caramel eyes dreamy and far away, as if he's in a trance. Then his lips are searching for mine and I feel the warmth of his breath as he slips a hand around my waist and pulls me against him.

"Jenna." When he says my name, his voice is husky, a man coming up for breath before diving under again. My heart races. Even in despair, Evan is beautiful. For a moment I long for the same thing, the sweet anesthetic of sexuality to pull me under and away from so much horror. I'm on the edge of surrender when a church bell chimes in the distance, pulling me out of my body and into my head. It would be so easy to lose myself in Evan. To try to rescue him. To try to rescue myself. But I know it won't work. Time to leave fairyland behind, Cinderella. Evan isn't my guy.

Liam wasn't either, and if I hadn't rushed into that relationship, I could have saved myself a lot of heartache.

I'll never jump in heart first again.

Gently, I push Evan away. "This won't help you. Trust me. I know." He looks at me, hurt. I think he's going to speak, but after a beat, he nods in understanding.

The limo pulls up in front of Dave's building. I knock on the glass. The driver lowers the partition.

"Take him straight home please." I gather my skirt around me and tuck the borrowed clutch under my arm. Then I push the door open and step onto the pavement in my now-scuffed silver shoes. The night air is cool and brisk.

"Thanks for an *almost* fairytale," I sigh and close the door behind me. It's midnight, time to step back into reality.

Chapter 33
Law & Order

Much to Dave's annoyance, I've gleefully discovered I'm never more than half an hour away from an episode of *Law & Order*. And since I'm technically still recovering from my trauma, he's been humoring me, tolerating the regular sound of a banging gavel in his living room. This episode is called "The Myth of Fingerprints" from the original series, season 12, where a fingerprint examiner provides false testimony. I already googled the episode and found it was based on Joyce Gilchrist, aka Black Magic, whose testimonies sent innocent men to prison.

As I watch, I pack a box for Tyler: socks, T-shirts, beef jerky, cheese sticks, paper, envelopes, magazines, soap, and cigarettes, though I really wish he'd quit smoking. Ever since Tyler helped with the investigation, he's been better. I made him promise not to give up. Together, we'll find out what really happened in Bell River.

A week has gone by since the Faux Fur and Furry Friends Fête. Andrea Billingsworth came home to find her cats happily purring, her litter boxes spotless, and her wine cabinet replenished.

Dave's new relationship is going well. His date actually enjoyed the drama of having to race to feed the lizard.

I gave Nadir Rashid another little present from the FBI, a second shiny new thumb drive, courtesy of Cole Braedon. He was so thrilled, he declared me "wicked."

Evan sent me a postcard from the Deepak Chopra Center in California, where he went for the *Healing the Heart Retreat.* I'm secretly hoping after he experiences a little of the "emotional freedom" they talk about on their website, he might consider culinary school. Max, who is getting better at walking in a straight line every day, is bunking with me at Dave's until his master returns.

Mohammad and Fatima set up the "Cintia Ab El Malik Memorial Fund for the Progress of the Bedouin People" and began the difficult work of relocating the Zahar Tribe to a less pungent locale. I saw a haunting picture in the paper of the couple standing with Ali Kabir at Cintia's funeral, which I did not attend. They offered to fly me to The Kingdom on their private jet, and believe me, I was tempted. But I draw the funeral attendance line at people who try to murder me, although I wish Cintia well in the next world, should there be one.

And me? Well, after several conversations with both Denning and Wolfson, I've decided to accept an invitation into Wolfson's prestigious intern program. I'm pretty excited. I haven't been good at very many things in my life, but they both think I have "it"— what it takes to be a good detective. So I'm going all in on my degree in criminology and my plan to get my little brother out of jail.

Just as I finish packing Ty's box, the doorbell rings. I tap the intercom button.

"Yes?"

"Delivery for Jenna Stack."

"Great. Just leave it at the mailbox area."

I buzz him through the outer door.

The bell rings again.

"Instructions are to hand deliver."

"Okay."

I buzz him inside the building. A thread of panic prickles my skin. Should I be suspicious? A few minutes later, there's a knock on the door. I peep through the hole and see a scraggly bike courier dressed like a refugee from a skateboarding convention, with zig-zag glasses and a yellow day-glow windbreaker.

Good disguise—if he's here to kill me. I open the door a crack, leaving the chain on. If he's an assassin, the chain won't do me any good. But it makes me feel better. "Set it down next to the door."

With Cintia dead and the Krov called off, I know I'm being ridiculous. But it never hurts to be careful.

He sets a misshapen manila envelope down and slips a clipboard through the gap. The paper is blank. There isn't even a company name. I peek through the crack at him.

"Ran out of printed pages. Gotta get more at the office. It's cool. Just sign your name and the time."

I sign the paper and hand the clipboard back. Once he's back in the elevator, I slip the chain off and snatch the package from the hallway.

The front of the manila envelope says, *Jenna: Please review* in an elaborate cursive hand. I take a knife from the kitchen drawer, slice it open, and pull an official-looking paper out of the envelope. It's a lab report. Written on top is *Case Number 06-563281: Hair Analysis.*

I suck in my breath like I've been punched in the stomach. This is Tyler's case—I grab my keys and race out the door and down the stairs, the lab report still clutched in my hand.

As I burst onto the street. The messenger is just mounting his bike, about to take off.

"Wait! Wait! Who sent that package?"

He looks at me like I'm nuts and slips his shoes into the pedals.

"I dunno. I just deliver—"

I don't believe him.

"Bull! You didn't have me sign a real delivery sheet—you're running a side racket. Now tell me who gave you the package, or I'm calling your boss."

He stops, puts his feet on the asphalt.

"All right, all right. Some tough dude. Green eyes. He was smoking a black cigarette. He flagged me down outside our office. Paid me two hundred bucks to make the delivery. Scared the crap out of me, but I wasn't about to turn down the cash. Are we cool?"

I nod, and the kid shrugs and bikes off.

So, Cole Braedon is still in espionage mode. As I walk back upstairs, I think about the evidence that sent Tyler to prison in the first place. A block away from the murder scene, the police found a hoodie and stocking mask shoved in a trashcan. Coach Vitner's blood was on the hoodie, and seven hairs were found on the stocking. At the trial, a forensic expert testified that those hairs matched Tyler's. That one fact, along with a pile of circumstantial evidence, sent my brother to prison.

Back in Dave's apartment, I smooth out the paper and run my finger along a list of chemicals. Three stand out: testosterone, stanozolol, and nandrolone. Next to each one is the word DETECTED in bright red letters. I've never seen this report before. *Ever.* According to these test results, the infamous hairs in the stocking cap tested positive for *anabolic steroids.*

But that's impossible. Tyler never took steroids. I would have known. My heart starts to pound. According to this lab report, the hair in the stocking cap wasn't Tyler's hair at all. What I'm holding is new evidence. Evidence we didn't have during the trial. Lost?

Suppressed? Altered? Buried? I don't know, but I need to figure this out.

With a start, I realize something else. This is a clue to the real killer! Whoever murdered Coach Vitner was a steroid user. For the first time in a long time, I feel that little something Pandora managed to save in her box: *Hope.*

The manilla envelope catches my attention again. There's a faint, square shape at one corner. What is that? I reach inside and pull out a small box tied with a ribbon. I open it. Inside is an Irish Claddagh ring, two silver hands holding a crowned heart. A small, printed note reads:

Heart pointed out if you're single. Heart pointed in if your heart has been captured.

I consider the instructions. Then I slip the ring on, smiling, with the heart pointed out—at least for now.

More From Hanna Wren

Can't wait to find out what happens next?

Turn the page to read the first chapter of Jenna Stack's next thrilling adventure. *A Dangerous Favor is available now in paperback and ebook!*

Internship Proposal
University of Manhattan
Name: Jenna Stack
GPA: 4.0
Degree Concentration: Criminology / Minor in
Sociology

Proposed Placement:
Bell River Police Department, Eastmoor County,
New York

Project Description:
I want to intern with local law enforcement in
a small-town setting where I can learn through
hands-on experience while applying practical
knowledge to various tasks and situations. I
have selected my hometown of Bell River, New
York. In addition to meeting the small-town
criteria, the crime rate in the county is
higher than those of similar size and
demographics in the region. I plan to study
county archives and community dynamics to
ascertain the causes of this anomaly.
Additionally, there are practical
considerations, such as familiarity with the
area and affordable living arrangements.

Project Duration: Winter Quarter

I pull the cover sheet for my Intern Proposal out of the printer and clip it into a folder. At eleven a.m. this morning, I have my quarterly evaluation with Professor Wolfson, head of the Criminology Department at the University of Manhattan. I plan to submit my proposal to him then, *in person.*

I've filled out all the paperwork, taken the required courses, and submitted a Student Enrichment application to the Bell River Police Department. If BRPD accepts me and Wolfson approves, I'll start my internship in twelve weeks. The truth is, I can't afford to be turned down—my brother's life depends on it.

For inspiration, I've propped my crime board up on the chair in my bedroom. Red, Yellow, and Blue threads crisscross the surface. Like a colorful spider's web, they connect the evidence that convicted my brother of first-degree murder. But Tyler is innocent, and I plan to prove it.

For one thing, I have a new piece of evidence, a lab report that was never presented at Tyler's trial. But to figure out exactly how this new information factors into the case, I'll need to search the police files where the murder occurred. My only chance to do that is from the inside. And I'll only get inside Bell River PD via one of Professor Wolfson's famous internships. He's already assured me I'm a shoo-in for the program. It's my choice of location that will pose a problem. I need to convince him that Bell River is the ideal location for this budding criminologist to hone her skills.

"Jenna?" A loud rap on the door startles me, and I almost spill my coffee. It's Dave, my best friend, roommate, and proud owner of *Tails of the City Pet Sitting Agency,* making him my part-time boss.

Instead of waiting for an answer, Dave barges right into my room. He looks polished and put together, as always, even when invading my personal space. Today he's wearing a light orange polo shirt accentuating his tan and slim-fit-khaki pants that flatter his physique. His styled blond hair appears effortlessly disheveled, and he's cultivated a light stubble on his cheeks and chiseled jawline, giving his face a less pretty, more rugged look. His high-voltage smile fades when he sees what I've been up to this morning.

Dave disapproves of my crime board. He thinks I spend too much time staring at the same notes, colored strings, and photos with nothing to show for my efforts. I try to shove the offending materials under my bed, but it's too late.

"Oh, Jenna, what am I going to do with you?" He scowls at the enormous piece of foam board balanced awkwardly in my arms. "That thing is a crime against your mental health. And your room looks like an actual crime scene. I can't even stand being in here. Come on." He motions for me to follow him.

I have to admit, my room is a mess. Clothes are scattered all over the floor, and the desk is piled high with papers and empty coffee mugs. Between school, two jobs, and working on Tyler's case, I don't have much time for housekeeping.

"I can't talk right now." I nudge some dirty clothes under the bed with my foot. "I'm getting ready for my evaluation with Professor Wolfson."

"Well, I'm on a tight schedule, and there's work stuff to go over. So do you think you could make some time?"

"I *really* need to figure out how to talk Wolfson into letting me intern in Bell River *before* I meet with him. I know you don't approve…"

Dave's expression softens.

"Honey, I know you're trying to help Tyler. But do you really think spending three months working at that backwoods police department in that awful town is such a great idea?"

"It's the only lead I've got, Dave. I *really* need you to be supportive."

"Okay. Okay," He throws up his hands in surrender. "But right now, I *really* need you to focus on the business. It'll just take a minute."

Our eyes meet, and suddenly, I feel terrible. When my relationship blew up six months ago, Dave took me in, no questions asked. He gave me a place to live and nursed me through the heartache. All he asked for in return, all he continues to ask, is for some help running his business.

Feeling contrite, I follow Dave into the living room, which, since I moved into his spare room and former office, has become the nerve center of Tails of the City. Out of the corner of my eye, I spot three enormous pieces of brand new, matching luggage inside the front door.

Oh no! Today is the day Dave leaves on a long overdue, much needed, Parisian vacation with his recently acquired, glamorous boyfriend, Matty Cooper.

"Oh Dave, I forgot you leave today. I'm so sorry!"

"Yeah, I figured," he brushes it off with a shrug. "Give me five minutes to get you up to speed, and then you can get back to *Operation Small Town Invasion*. Okay? Matty is literally on his way."

"Absolutely! I'm all yours."

Dave points to a massive bulletin board with a map of Manhattan covered in colored push pins. "These are the pet sitters assigned to various clients. Gary is out of town until tomorrow. Then he'll take care of Mrs. Brochelle and Erik Tran. His pins are green. If anything new comes in, ask him first. He's always looking to pick up extra work. Gina's watching Matty's place and has a few simple dog walking routes. Her pins are yellow. Sandy is covering all of her usual clients. She's red. All you have to do is make sure everything runs smoothly."

"Got it," I reassure him. "Everything will be fine."

"I left a list of contacts in case of special requests. The regulars have your info, but don't forget to check this too." He hands me the official Tails of the City cell phone.

"You're not bringing this with you?"

"No, Jenna. I'm going on vacation, and you are in charge. You can handle this, right?"

Dave built *Tails of the City Pet Sitting Agency* into a thriving business in just two and a half years. Dog walking, pet meal prep and meds, exotic animal care, full-service apartment sitting, even pet travel arrangements, and the occasional errand; whatever the client needs, Tails of the City handles it well and discreetly. But he's had zero downtime since the whole thing started.

So, when Matty went from client to boyfriend and invited him on vacation, Dave jumped. Still, leaving his business for even a short time must be nerve-wracking.

I nod firmly. "I will not let you down."

His broad shoulders relax, but only for a few seconds.

"Oh! One more thing." He plucks a large manila envelope off of his crowded desk. There's a name written on the front in Dave's precise handwriting: *Natalie Swanson*. No address or sign of a postage stamp. Uh oh.

"What's that?"

"Some paperwork for a client. A legal document." Dave quickly scrawls an address in the east 40s under Natalie Swanson's name and hands the envelope to me. "I was supposed to deliver this myself, but I ran out of time. Matty upgraded our tickets, and we're on an earlier flight." His eyes light up at the mention of his considerate boyfriend.

"Okay." I set the envelope down. "I'll do it tomorrow."

"No!" Dave snatches it up again. "Natalie needs this letter

ASAP, and I promised. She's a total sweetheart, and she's in a terrible situation."

I raise an eyebrow skeptically. Dave can be a bit dramatic at times.

"Seriously, she's in the middle of an ugly divorce. Her husband is a lawyer and a total prick. He kicked her out and moved the girlfriend in practically the next day. He even had Natalie followed by a private eye and is threatening to make her look bad in court. Worst of all, he took her babies."

"Her children?" I stare at the envelope in Dave's hand, horrified.

"No, her *dogs*. It's a pet custody case. I'm trying to help her."

"Pet custody?" I've never heard of a pet custody case, but it does explain how Dave got involved.

"Her ex is going out of town, so she gets Olive and Pepper for a few days. But she needs this document to make it official, and she's very anxious." Dave thrusts the envelope at me. "So, you need to bring it to her *today*, Jenna! Before you do anything else!"

I'm a little suspicious of Dave's explanation. It seems weird that someone would need a legal document to watch their own dogs. And I have my own problems.

"I just can't. Not today. I need to prepare—"

There's a sudden loud buzzing noise. Dave rushes over to the front door.

"Who is it?" he calls nervously into the intercom.

"Who do you think, silly?" Matty replies.

Dave triggers the door release and waves for me to join him. We stand side-by-side while Matty makes his way up in the elevator. I feel ridiculous like I'm in a receiving line to greet royalty. But it is sweet that Dave is always so excited to see his boyfriend.

Moments later, Matty Cooper walks through the door wearing casual slacks, a black T-shirt, and a fashionable, but well-worn, khaki jacket with dozens of pockets. His short, dark hair is freshly cut, and his beard is neatly trimmed. He is dragging a single, rolling, carry-on suitcase. The overall look is travel chic and ready to go.

"Hey, Jenna." Matty gives me a warm hug. "Thanks for watching the shop." Then he turns to Dave, "Ready?"

"Yes." Dave points to his pristine and excessive luggage.

Matty cringes.

"You know we're not *moving* to Paris?"

Dave ignores Matty's teasing and adds, "We just have to make a quick stop in the forties."

"No way," Matty shakes his head. "We don't have time."

"I'm sorry," Dave throws up his hands. "But I promised, and Jenna's just *too busy*."

They both look at me. Damn you, Dave!

"Please, Jenna," Matty tilts his head hopefully.

"Pretty please," Dave coos, suppressing a smirk.

"Fine! I'll do it."

Dave grabs me and kisses me on both cheeks, French style.

"You're the best! Tails of the City is in your hands, Mon Cherie! Whatever you do, please don't drop it!"

"I won't let you down. I promise. Now go have fun!"

Dave blows me an exaggerated kiss and shouts, "Au revoir!"

Matty maneuvers the luggage down the hallway as Dave runs to catch up. I shut the door behind them and smile to myself. I should be mad at Dave for putting me on the spot. But I'm not. Knowing he's happy and off on a romantic adventure feels good. And sure, dropping off Natalie Swanson's paperwork is inconvenient. But the apartment is on the way. I can make a quick stop.

My stomach rumbles, reminding me I haven't eaten yet. But with an extra task on my plate, there's no time to waste. I race around the apartment, gathering my things - backpack, internship proposal, laptop, my phone, the Tails of the City phone, the envelope for Natalie Swanson, a protein bar, and an apple.

Then I make sure everything's turned off, lock the door behind me and head out. I'll have to eat and rehearse my conversation with Professor Wolfson on the subway. I've got to find a way to convince him to send me to Bell River.

About Hanna Wren

Hanna Wren is the pen name authors Amy Eyrie and Alix Sloan use when writing together.

Visit HannaWren.com to learn more about them and find Hanna Wren on social media. While you're there, join the Hanna Wren mailing list for updates and freebies.

And if you enjoyed this book, please help other readers discover the Jenna Stack Mysteries by leaving a review on Amazon, Goodreads, or any place you review or talk about books.